# FESTIVALS, FUNNEL CAKES & FELONIES

## A Dogwood Springs Cozy Mystery

SALLY BAYLESS

Paperback ISBN: 978-1-946034-31-1

Kimberlin Belle Publishing LLC

Contact: admin@kimberlinbelle.com



Cover art by DLR Cover Designs, www.dlrcoverdesigns.com.

# Chapter One



*Sunday, April 28*

"C'MON, BELLA." I opened the car door wider.

My five-year-old golden retriever gave an excited woof and scrambled out into the parking lot near the stage at the Dogwood Springs Fairgrounds.

"Darcy's already here." I pointed to a navy SUV, one of two other cars in the lot. "We'd better hurry." I leaned down to snap on Bella's leash and caught my reflection in the window.

*Yikes.* Driving with the windows open might not have been the best idea. I glanced in the side mirror and smoothed down my shoulder-length brown hair. Then I brushed a bit of dog hair off my festival volunteer T-shirt.

Once I was presentable, I gave Bella a pat, and we started toward the big picnic area. That's where I was supposed to meet Darcy Jackson, the local banker and amateur photographer who was running the Dogwood Queen contest.

The sun warmed my bare arms, and I drew in a deep breath of fresh air. With luck, the weather for the festival weekend would be as nice as today's. It was a perfect Missouri spring day, sunny with a predicted high of seventy-five, and the fairgrounds area, which was shaped like a long half oval, looked lovely. Bounded by Hartley Road on the south and the curve of the Dogwood River in other directions, it was scattered with clusters of dogwood trees, all in full bloom.

Last year during the festival, I had accepted my current job as director of the Dogwood Springs History Museum but hadn't yet moved to town. This time, I was not only one of two hundred local volunteers, but I would also proudly wear a gold name badge that said, "Libby Ballard, Festival Steering Committee."

I couldn't wait to be part of this event that meant so much to the community. Two and a half days of crafts, live music, food, and drink, all wrapped into a wonderful weekend that drew in tourists and raised money for a local charity.

As part of my duties, today I was to assist Darcy in getting all the Dogwood Queen finalists lined up to pose for a promotional photo. We'd arranged to meet at a quarter 'til three, fifteen minutes before the girls were due to arrive.

Bella and I walked past the indoor restrooms, and as we neared the smaller of the two grassy vendor areas, my dog stopped to sniff near one of its paved paths.

"Hey, Bella, no time for that," I protested, as she began digging in the grass. "We need to meet Darcy. You're supposed to calm any girls who might be nervous about the photo, not get mud all over them." The last thing I wanted was to literally make a mess of this volunteer task.

After all, the festival wasn't only important to me as a volunteer. It was also part of my day job. Since I'd started my new position, I'd worked hard to make the Dogwood Springs History Museum a success. We would have a tent at the festival, highlighting some of our most popular displays, giving the history of the town's abundance of dogwood trees, and engaging visitors in a guess-the-antiques contest. The more successful the festival was, the more people would see our exhibit and hopefully later visit the museum.

As added motivation for me personally, my ex-husband —the man who'd cheated on me, divorced me, and been responsible for me losing my previous job at a prestigious historic home in Philadelphia—would be dropping by the museum on his way to a family reunion in Oklahoma. Was it any wonder I wanted our little local museum to be bursting at the seams with visitors when he showed up?

*Hold on. Bella wasn't beside me.*

I turned and found she'd spotted a small toad.

"Bella, leave Mr. Toad alone. You're probably scaring him."

She cocked her head and peered at the creature again, then trotted back over to my side.

"Good girl." I scratched between her ears.

She rubbed her head against my leg.

Such a sweetie. I'd adopted Bella right after I moved to Dogwood Springs, and it had been one of the best decisions of my life. No matter what, she made me feel like the most important person in the world. She brought joy to my good days, and when life threw problems my way, she seemed to sense my mood and gave me even more affection. Not only was she pure love, but she was also incredibly smart. I was grateful to have her in my life.

We passed the smaller vendor area and neared the big picnic spot, that area that would become the wine and beer garden for the festival and the place where I was supposed to meet Darcy.

But she wasn't there.

*Hmmm.* "Maybe she got tired of waiting for us, Bella." I pulled my phone from my oversized purse. No, we weren't late. And Darcy and I weren't close friends. I didn't have her number, so I couldn't call her to check. "Let's go to the little waterfall where she wanted to take the photo." Maybe she was figuring out how to handle the lighting under the trees.

I gave Bella's leash a gentle tug, and we headed toward the river. Its small waterfall was a perfect spot for a photo.

I peered ahead toward the trees by the river's banks. Darcy had brown eyes and long, wavy, dark brown hair. She tended to wear bright colors, especially red.

I was sure I'd catch a glimpse of something red through the trees.

But I didn't see her anywhere.

Bella and I walked a bit farther, and the path split. One branch continued toward the river, and the other led to the larger vendor area and, past that, to the main parking lot near the barns.

Harry Myers, the festival's director, appeared from around a cluster of trees and hurried toward me.

"Good morning, Libby!" he called, giving me a friendly wave.

I waved back.

A widower in his early sixties, Harry had retired as a bigwig at a major phone company and moved to Dogwood Springs about the time I'd come here. When the previous festival director became ill, he'd taken over working with the all-volunteer staff as if he'd been born for the role. Clearly, community service had long been part of his life.

Harry had a fringe of white hair, blue eyes, perfect white teeth, and the quick, easy gait of a man in great health. As usual, today he wore track pants, tennis shoes, and one of his many polo shirts. He seemed to have a huge collection of them, each from a different golf course that I'd never heard of. I was no golfer, but even if I were, I doubt I could afford to play his favorite courses.

"I've been so impressed, Harry, with the way every-thing's going for the festival," I said as he came up. "It seems like the changes you've made will really draw the tourists."

He'd offered all sorts of new ideas and given volunteers a lot of freedom, encouraging them to try out different jobs if they wanted. From what other volunteers had told me, the previous director, Sylvia Snodgrass, had run the festival with an iron hand and done things exactly the same way for fifteen years.

Bella crossed in front of me, eager to greet Harry.

"Just some ideas I picked up from other events I've done." Harry patted Bella's head and smiled down at her. "I'm proud of your contributions, Libby. With your logical mind, attention to detail, and organizational skills, I can see why the museum has been doing so well."

Pride and delight rippled through me. Harry was a wonderful manager, and Dogwood Springs was lucky the festival was in such good hands. Speaking of the festival, where was the person in charge of the queen contest? "Harry, have you seen Darcy? I spotted her car in the parking lot near the stage, but I haven't seen her."

"No, I got here about fifteen minutes ago, hoping to talk to her and see how the photo shoot goes. My car's in the main lot, near the barns." He jerked a thumb behind him. "But I got tied up in a phone call with one of the vendors from out of town, a guy named Jimbo. He had some questions about the electrical setup."

"Let's look for her near the waterfall. That's where she plans to take the photo," I said.

Harry agreed, and we walked toward the river.

Bella wandered back close to Harry and sniffed at his hands in a way that made me wonder if he'd eaten a burger for lunch before he arrived at the park.

I pulled Bella back to my side just as we got a full view of the Dogwood River.

The stream was only about twenty-five yards across, and

the water was crystal clear. Dogwoods and redbud lined the banks, with taller cedars and oaks providing shade. The waterfall itself was about eight feet tall, and the water whooshed as it tumbled over chunks of limestone, swirling into a frothy white pool before flowing downstream. Such a lovely place.

But I still didn't see Darcy.

I turned to Harry. "Do you think she took a different path and went back to her car to get something?"

"Maybe." He shrugged.

Suddenly, Bella barked and pulled hard on her leash.

She tugged me up the hill, and Harry kept pace as we went up a rise to the top of the waterfall. The ripple of delight I'd felt earlier turned to ice in my chest.

There, above the falls, something mostly submerged in the water was caught on a branch.

Something that had long, dark hair.

## Chapter Two

BELLA PULLED AT HER LEASH, desperate to dive into the water to help, but Harry had already kicked off his tennis shoes.

"Call 911!" he shouted to me. He waded into the shallow edge of the river and hit the deeper water with a splash.

"Help!" I yelled over my shoulder as I dug my phone from my purse, hoping the queen finalists and their parents might be arriving. I dialed 911, while listening for someone to shout in response to my cry.

But no one did.

A moment later, though, a young blond man wearing the neon-yellow T-shirt of the Dogwood Springs Parks Department ran up, followed by Madison Thompson, a receptionist at the vet's office where I took Bella, and her redheaded teenage daughter, Zoe. Seconds later, Bryce Parker, a vet in the same office as well as Darcy's fiancé, also sprinted down the path toward us. A man with ash-brown hair and a receding hairline was right behind him.

The 911 operator came on the line, and I explained what had happened.

Harry moved closer to shore, pulling the body behind him. When he neared, I was able to spot a face.

*Darcy.* A chill ran through me.

"Help me get her out!" Harry shouted. "The water is freezing."

Bryce waded onto the ledge and leaned out to grasp Darcy's shoulder. Then he, Madison, and the guy from the parks department carried her out of the water and laid her on the grass.

"Is she ... alive?" I moved closer, trying to see. "911 says help is on the way."

Madison's blond hair fell forward as she felt for a pulse at Darcy's neck. She looked back at me and shook her head. "I don't think so, but I'll try CPR." She repositioned Darcy.

I saw the wound on the back of Darcy's head and inhaled sharply.

Madison took off her lightweight hoodie, wrapped it around Darcy's head, and began chest compressions.

Bryce had frozen, his hazel eyes glazed as if he were stunned. After a second, he scrubbed a hand through his wavy hair and took turns doing CPR with Madison.

"Is she alive?" the 911 operator asked me.

I blinked and refocused on the phone call.

"I don't know," I said, my voice shaky. "Two people are

trying CPR, but she's got a giant, bloody wound on the back of her head."

"I'll go meet the paramedics and direct them here," the park staffer said. He dashed back down the path.

Bryce and Madison continued CPR.

The rest of us stood nearby, watching helplessly.

I saw no indication that Darcy was responding.

The 911 operator stayed on the line with me, checking in every now and then to ask if I was okay as we waited for the first responders.

*Okay* was a relative term. With so many people around, I knew I wasn't in any danger. But after seeing that deep gash on Darcy's head, I felt jittery. Maybe that was shock. Or the sneaking suspicion that her injury might not have been an accident. The position of the wound was so high on the back of her head, it was hard to imagine how it could have been caused by a fall.

Either way, I wasn't the only one affected by the situation.

The man with ash-brown hair, who looked to be in his late forties, kept fisting and releasing his hands. Zoe twisted a long lock of her wavy red hair, fear in her big blue eyes.

Zoe was a sweet girl who had been an early queen candidate but didn't make the finals. I'd seen her a couple of times with Zeke, the teenage nephew of my best friend and upstairs neighbor, Cleo Anderson.

Always attuned to human emotions, Bella moved closer to Zoe and rubbed her head against the girl's leg.

Harry, too, must have sensed Zoe's unease. He wrung

the water from the hem of his golf shirt and patted her shoulder.

Zoe let out a shaky sigh and rested a hand on Bella's back.

Moments later, we heard sirens, and then an ambulance and a police car cut across the grass.

Two paramedics climbed out of the ambulance and ran toward us. Madison and Bryce backed away, and the paramedics immediately began caring for Darcy.

"Does anyone know what happened here?" Officer Tate, a calm, capable guy in his thirties who I'd met a few times, walked over from the police car with a young female officer I didn't know.

Harry stepped forward. "Libby and I found her. I got her out of the water, but..." He made a feeble gesture as if he feared the same thing I did—that we had arrived too late.

"I was supposed to meet Darcy and help her take photos of the Dogwood Queen finalists," I said. "They should be arriving any minute now."

"No photographs today," Officer Tate said. Then he sent his partner to work with other officers to direct anyone else who arrived at the park to go home.

Officer Tate turned back to the rest of us and gestured over his shoulder. "Let's go over to that picnic area."

"Good idea." Detective John Harper, a short, heavyset man in his fifties, strode down the path. He stared at Darcy for a few seconds, then quickly took command. "Let's give the paramedics room to work, and I'll get some information from each of the witnesses."

He looked at me, and his eyebrows—considerably darker than his salt-and-pepper buzz cut—bunched together. After the interactions we'd had during previous investigations I'd somehow gotten involved with, I could almost hear the lecture that was coming. "Libby Ballard," he said. "What are you doing here?"

"I'm on the festival steering committee," I said. "I was here to help Darcy with some promotional photos."

"Uh-huh." His mouth flattened into a line before he led me back to the big picnic area and gestured to a table in the far corner. Some of the tables were shaded by large oaks, so I was grateful the detective picked a table in the sun, as I still felt cold.

He scratched Bella's ears, then sat across from me and pulled a small notebook from the pocket of his blue dress shirt. "So, tell me what happened."

Bella let out a sigh and settled herself on the concrete floor of the picnic area.

I briefly explained how Bella and I had arrived at the fairgrounds, run into Harry, and walked with him to the waterfall, hoping to find Darcy. "Do you think there might have been a wet spot on the path, and she slipped and hit her head?" I hoped my suspicions about Darcy's wound were wrong.

He gave me a skeptical look, then his radio squawked, and his frown deepened. "The paramedics weren't able to save her."

My heart sank, and I sat silent for a long moment. I hadn't been close to Darcy, but it was hard to believe she was dead. Only two days ago, we'd been at a steering committee meeting together.

Detective Harper laid his pen down beside his pad. "Libby, it's great you're helping with the festival, but I can't believe you've managed to end up at the scene of what looks like another suspicious death."

Wow. So it wasn't only me who suspected Darcy might have been attacked. I knew she wasn't well liked, but still... "Her injury certainly wasn't my fault."

"I'm not saying you were responsible in any way," the detective said. "I just wish—for your own safety—that you hadn't been here today."

A shiver ran down my spine as I realized I might have narrowly missed running into a murderer.

"How well did you know Darcy?" the detective asked.

"Not that well. Just a few conversations at the steering committee meetings."

"Did she ever mention someone had been bothering her?"

I thought for a moment and shook my head. We probably weren't close enough that she would have shared that type of information. "No, but I just remembered something. There were only two cars in the small lot by the stage when I got here today. Darcy's and one other. There can't have been that many cars in the other lot. If we can find out who was parked in each lot, we could probably narrow down the list of suspects." Cars couldn't park on Hartley Road because it was a major thoroughfare. Across the road from the fairgrounds was a ravine, and the other sides of the grounds were bounded by the river.

"Libby, you shouldn't get involved." He scrubbed a hand over his hair. "You've taken far too many risks in the past." For a moment, his eyes softened. "You're a good person, a valuable member of the community. I'm proud of you for helping at the festival, but I do not want you being nosy and trying to figure out what happened here."

"But—"

"No," he cut me off. "We'll wait to see what the coroner says, but there's a good chance I've now got a murder to solve—in addition to a case involving someone scamming elderly residents out of their life savings. I do not need to be worried that you'll end up dead as well."

Okay, fine. There wasn't anything I could say to that. So I had happened to get involved in investigating a few suspicious deaths since I moved to Dogwood Springs, and each time, I'd figured out the murderer before Detective Harper. It wasn't my fault I had a strong sense of justice and enjoyed solving puzzles, whether they were crosswords, mystery novels, or mysteries in real life. And maybe I was a little bit stubborn. Granted, there had been a couple of close calls, but I'd never intentionally put myself in danger.

A rabbit hopped by. Bella jumped to her feet, her body tense as she watched the bunny bound over to a patch of clover near the stage.

The same stage where bands were supposed to play on Friday.

"Detective, let's say you learn for sure Darcy was murdered. What will that mean for the festival?"

His jaw tightened. "At this point, I don't know."

## Chapter Three

I GAVE a gentle tug to Bella's leash and walked with her to another picnic table as Detective Harper began talking with the others. First, he spoke with Madison and Zoe together, then individually with Bryce and Harry. Next, he interviewed the park worker—whose name I just happened to overhear was Aaron Eckhart—and finally, the man with ash-brown hair, who I learned was Cameron Sidwell.

Unfortunately, once Detective Harper started asking each person for more than their name, every single one of them spoke more quietly. I couldn't move closer without making it obvious I was trying to listen in. The only other information I caught was that Cameron was worried that his stepdaughter, one of the queen candidates who was somewhere at the fairgrounds, might be in danger. The detective radioed one of his officers and assured Cameron his stepdaughter was safe, but the man still looked worried.

Finally, Detective Harper finished his interviews and

said we all could leave. He directed Officer Tate to escort us to the parking lots, then walked back toward the waterfall.

When Bella and I reached the parking lot by the stage, an officer stood watch. I learned that the other car in the lot besides mine and Darcy's, an upscale black sedan with dark windows, belonged to Cameron. His stepdaughter, Noelle, climbed out of the car as soon as he drew near and began complaining about how long she'd had to wait. In my opinion, she'd been lucky. I wasn't sure where she had been when we found Darcy's body, but it was better that she hadn't witnessed the scene.

"Ready to go home, Bella?" I opened the passenger-side door of my Camry.

She hopped in, always eager for a ride, and the two of us headed out.

Ten minutes later, we arrived at the white frame house where I rented the downstairs. The two-story home had been built in 1900, and even when it was new, it hadn't been anything fancy. But it fit my budget, was an easy walk to the museum, and had some history. I'd found the original owner's initials on the underside of the hand-carved mantel shortly after I moved in. And recently I'd discovered a stack of *Life* magazines from the 1940s, way back on a high shelf in my bedroom closet.

As I turned into the narrow driveway, I spotted Cleo on the porch. Once I'd parked on my side of the detached garage, I walked around to the front of the house, grateful to be able to talk to her after what had happened at the fairgrounds.

From the day I'd moved in, Cleo had treated me like the best friend she'd always longed for. I couldn't have asked for anyone more loyal and supportive.

"Hey, Libby, look what I've got." She pointed to a flat of orange, rust, purple, and yellow pansies and two empty flowerpots that flanked the porch steps. The blossoms smiled up at me like happy faces. "It's way past time to fill these two pots I bought on clearance last fall."

Bella hurried over to say hello, and Cleo bent down to rub her ears.

Other than our ages—with Cleo just two years younger than me—we didn't have a lot in common. She was tall and had big brown eyes and a blond pixie cut with long bangs. I was average height with green eyes and brown hair that curled under at my shoulders. She wore oversized glasses and bright colors and kept up with the latest fashion trends. I stuck with classics and, when I wanted to polish my look, added my great-great-grandmother's pearls. Cleo was vivacious and a bit loud compared to my quieter personality. And for the past ten months, when we'd shared this house on Elm Street, I was the one who tested smoke detectors and bought salt to have on hand in case of ice while Cleo decorated the front porch and planted flowers. She had a love of crafts and an artistic eye that showed in both her decorating and in the hairstyles she created in the salon she ran.

"The flowers are lovely," I said. "But..."

Cleo frowned, and she shut off the music she'd been playing on her phone. "What's wrong?"

"I've got some bad news."

She gestured to the two Adirondack chairs on the porch, and we sat down. "Was there a problem with the photo shoot?"

I shifted in my chair. "Sort of. Darcy's dead."

Cleo drew in a sharp breath.

"Most likely murdered," I added.

Cleo's eyes grew wide. She covered her mouth with one hand and sat back in her chair.

Bella walked over to Cleo and rested her head on Cleo's thigh.

As kindly as I could, I explained what had happened.

"Oh, I'm so sorry you had to be the one to find her." Cleo pressed her lips together. "Poor Darcy. Her poor family. And poor Bryce. They only set a wedding date in the past month. He has to be devastated."

"He did look very upset." I should have known Cleo's thoughts would quickly turn to Bryce. Although she was currently dating a local pediatrician, she and Bryce had been high school sweethearts. Cleo ended the relationship before they graduated but later regretted it.

Personally, now that I'd gotten past the initial shock, I had to admit I had mixed feelings about Darcy. She had certainly worked hard to make the queen contest a positive experience for the high school girls, and I had a feeling she'd been good at her job as a loan officer at Dogwood State Bank. But even though I couldn't picture anything she might have done to deserve being killed, I couldn't really say that I'd expected us to become friends outside the steering committee. Something about her hadn't made me want to spend extra time with her.

Cleo, on the other hand, had thoroughly disliked her. According to Cleo, Darcy was selfish and thought she was better than everyone else.

A niggle of tension ran through my stomach. Thinking someone was stuck-up was no reason for murder, but spending years pining away for the man who was Darcy's fiancé might be. "How, uh, how long were you out shopping for the pansies?"

"An hour or so, why?"

"I know you'd never kill anyone, but you disliked Darcy for years, and Detective Harper has come to some crazy conclusions in the past."

Cleo waved my concerns away with a slightly muddy hand. "Before I was at the greenhouse, I went to lunch with my parents at La Villetta to celebrate Mom's birthday. And before that, we were at church. Detective Harper is never going to pin this on me."

The tension in my stomach eased. "Good."

Cleo sat silent for a moment, then leaned forward. "What's this going to mean for the festival?"

"Detective Harper said he didn't know."

"Wow. We've had the festival since before I was born," Cleo brushed some of the dirt off her hands. "The money that's raised is important."

I nodded. After expenses, all proceeds from the gate and the locally provided food and drinks went to the Good Neighbors Fund, which helped students in need. The fund was overseen by a committee of local public-school teachers. Originally, the fund was used for items that teachers might pay for out of pocket, such as school supplies or a winter coat for a student. Eventually, the festival had grown enough to cover those expenses, plus three nice college scholarships for local students.

"I can't imagine canceling it now, only five days before," I said. "But I guess if the police believe the public is in danger…"

"Yeah. Better in the long run to cancel than to risk someone else getting killed." Cleo tipped her head to one side. "Are you going to call your ex-husband and tell him not to come?"

I rubbed my chin. "Maybe. I think I'll wait a day or two and see what happens. If the police arrest someone right away, there's no reason for Reggie not to drop by Dogwood Springs on the way to his family reunion."

I should have been completely over what happened with my ex—especially since I was dating a great guy, Sam Collins—but I wasn't. I felt a bit of dread about seeing Reggie again, but it paled next to the desire for him to see how well I'd recovered after he crushed my life back in Philadelphia.

Should I tell him not to come? I wasn't sure. Maybe after the shock of finding Darcy's body wore off, I'd know what to do.

Thoughts of Darcy's death poured into my mind as soon as I woke up the next morning. Luckily, I had my sweet dog to distract me.

I let Bella out and fed her, then showered and pulled on dress pants and a collared shirt as she gobbled down her breakfast. While I ate my own breakfast and drank a strong mug of Yorkshire black tea, Bella came to my side. She looked up at me with her big, brown eyes as if to let me know that—in spite of what had happened to Darcy—the world was still filled with good people. And, of course, good dogs. I gently stroked her back, feeling my unease fall away.

When I stood, she trotted over to where I kept her leash hanging in the kitchen. She nudged the lower end until it fell to the floor. Then she picked it up in her mouth, carried it over, and dropped it at my feet.

"You don't want to take a walk, do you, Bella?"

She gazed at me, her expression still full of love, but there might also have been a subtle message that I should hurry up.

"All right." I chuckled, put on my tennis shoes, and grabbed a light jacket.

The two of us headed out onto Elm Street. Bella turned to the right, ready for our regular walk to Thirteenth Street and back, but I paused first to gaze up and down the street.

In both directions, each yard contained at least one white dogwood tree, and they were all in bloom. The sweet scent of my neighbor's lilacs filled the air, and although an occasional car drove past, I mostly heard birds calling to each other, happy to greet the day.

It would be a shame if all the tourists stayed away from the Dogwood Festival this year. Everything looked so beautiful. And from what I had heard, many of the visitors looked forward to attending every spring.

Plus, the festival committee had so much planned.

Starting Friday morning at nine, people would wander among tents offering balloon animals, homemade candles, face painting, handcrafted jewelry, and every other craft item imaginable. They could even buy T-shirts, ball caps, tea towels, book bags, and mugs emblazoned with the festival logo.

If they got hungry, they'd find tasty treats from local vendors selling hot dogs, burgers, nachos, funnel cake, cotton candy, and frosted sugar cookies shaped like dogwood blossoms, as well as out-of-town vendors providing specialty food items. If they got thirsty, in addition to bottled water and soda, festivalgoers could buy fresh-squeezed lemonade or sample craft brews and wine from the local winery.

And after dinner, live music would fill the air, with three acts each evening, including a '70's tribute band I couldn't wait to see.

Granted, most people around my age, thirty-three, were more interested in current music than in bands from the 1970s. As a historian, though, I preferred things a little older, and for music that meant rock-and-roll classics. I was already hoping the tribute band would play some of my favorite songs.

All in all, if there hadn't just been a murder, the festival should have been fantastic.

But for all I knew it could be canceled.

I sighed and glanced ahead at the older homes that lined Elm Street. Between Fourth and Fifth Streets, where Cleo and I lived, many of the houses were rentals. The farther south Bella and I walked, the more upscale the houses became, and the more well-tended the yards. By around Eighth, the houses were almost all privately owned, and the neighbors were more competitive in their efforts to have the nicest yard. One house in particular always caught my eye. Right now, in addition to a large dogwood, the yard was bursting with light and dark pink peonies.

As I admired them, the front door opened. To my surprise, Harry walked out.

"Harry, good morning," I said. "You're out early."

"I'm an early riser, been up for hours. But I'm glad I happened to look out and see you. I plan to contact all the steering committee members today."

"I didn't realize you lived here." I gestured to the land-scaping. "This is one of the prettiest houses on the street. Your peonies are gorgeous."

"I can't take any credit for them, of course. They were planted years ago, but they are lovely." Harry reached down to pat Bella, but she seemed more interested in a bug on the sidewalk. He looked back up at me. "I talked with Detective Harper at seven this morning."

My shoulders tensed. "Is there news?"

"Big news. The festival is a go. The police have a strong suspect, unrelated to the festival."

"That's wonderful!" Why, it sounded like Detective Harper had the case practically solved. "Now everything can go ahead as planned, and the Good Neighbor Fund can be replenished."

"Replenished and more, if I have anything to do with it," Harry said.

I beamed at him. Wouldn't it be wonderful if Harry's first year as director—and mine in my much smaller role—turned out to be a record year for the festival? "Did Detective Harper say who the suspect was?"

"No, just that the police don't think the murder had anything to do with the festival."

"It's hard to imagine why someone would have wanted to kill Darcy." I ran a hand over the back of my neck. "Maybe it had something to do with her job. Financial issues can be hot buttons sometimes."

Harry's brows lowered. "I hadn't thought of that, but you may be right." His face grew somewhat brighter. "For now, all we know for sure is that we've got a festival to run."

"That's very good news, Harry. Very good news indeed."

## Chapter Four

AFTER OUR WALK, and once Bella was happily settled for the morning with a full water bowl, a new chew toy, and a dog biscuit I'd hidden for her to discover later, I changed into black flats, added my pearls, and packed up my big purse, making sure to include the tuna sandwich, chips, and grapes I planned for my lunch. I'd dash home at noon to let Bella out, but I preferred to nibble on my lunch at my desk rather than wolf it down. Once I had everything packed, I headed to the museum.

As I walked down Main Street, I enjoyed the window displays in the quaint shops and savored the aroma of what smelled like apple pie wafting out the door of the Dogwood Springs Bakery.

Although many of the shops wouldn't open until ten, the area was waking up. From its darling boutiques with colorful awnings to the pots of flowers outside every door, downtown Dogwood Springs was heavy on charm. Soon tourists would be nibbling on chocolate treats from Mimi's Candies or cookies from the Dogwood Springs Bakery, smelling the fresh Italian bread baking at La Villetta and contemplating a dinner reservation, or emerging from one of the shops with a larger-than-expected purchase.

It wasn't only downtown and the beautiful fairgrounds that were inviting. The hills surrounding the town were sprinkled with quaint bed and breakfasts, and an award-winning local winery was located just a mile away. In late April and early May, the town was wreathed in gorgeous dogwoods, and in the fall, the maple trees that lined almost every street in Dogwood Springs turned a gorgeous red.

Equally important, the whole community moved at a slower pace that was perfect for vacationers. Longtime residents claimed they'd actually seen tourists' shoulders relax as the town worked its magic.

At the far end of downtown, the Dogwood Springs History Museum stood tall and proud. Erected in 1920 as the private home of local businessman Charles Pennington, the two-story, white Greek Revival was built to impress. Even before Main Street was widened back in the 1940s, the house must have seemed ostentatious and too big for its lot. Today, thanks to hours of tender, loving care, the century-old building served the community well, welcoming school groups, townspeople, and tourists alike. Most importantly, the museum provided each visitor access to cultural history, a chance to learn more about the past, and insights to better understand themselves and their role in society. I was incredibly proud of the museum, and proud of how my staff and I, along with our volunteers, served our audience.

When he passed away, Charles Pennington had generously left his home and a large trust fund to the town for the purpose of providing a history museum. Thanks to that trust fund, unlike many small-town museums run completely by volunteers, we had a staff of three: me, Imani Jones, the education coordinator, and Rodney Grant, the curator.

I let myself in the back door, as we didn't open the front door to the public until ten, and I inhaled deeply. There was no fragrance I loved more than the combination of slightly musty papers, lemon furniture polish, and a hint of mothballs—the smell of a history museum.

I found Imani and Rodney sitting in what had once been the Pennington kitchen and was now our conference room. The only room in the building that had been updated other than the bathrooms, it included a kitchenette, a long table, and low-budget, 1980s' décor.

Rodney, a gray-haired, ruddy-faced man in his sixties, stood by the coffeemaker in his typical dress shirt and twill pants, spooning in a rich blend I recognized by the bag as his favorite. He was an excellent curator, a detail-oriented person who thought things over well before taking action.

Imani, a Black woman in her twenties, had the longest real eyelashes I'd ever seen and a closet full of vintage clothes. Today she wore an avocado pantsuit that I placed at about 1972. With her tall, slender build and her hair braided back into a bun, she looked like a model. Despite being the mom of a five-month-old, she also had the high energy needed as an education coordinator. Schoolkids loved her.

She took a few napkins from a drawer, set them by a box from the Dogwood Springs Bakery, and lifted the lid. "Hi, Libby. Today's special." She gestured toward the contents. "Apple cinnamon muffins with streusel crumble on top."

"I thought I smelled apple when I walked by the bakery this morning." I set a muffin on a napkin and put a mug of water in the microwave for tea.

Recently, the three of us had begun having early Monday morning meetings in the conference room to discuss the week ahead. Imani had suggested that we take turns bringing in a treat from the bakery. Rodney and I had wholeheartedly agreed.

When I looked back on how I'd kicked off Mondays at my job in Philadelphia—alone in my office, answering all the emails that had accumulated over the weekend—I appreciated my new position even more. What better way to start the week than enjoying tea and breakfast treats with my colleagues? Best of all, although Rodney had a dry, quiet wit, and Imani was more of a giggler, they each had a terrific sense of humor.

I bit into my muffin, which tasted even better than it smelled. The sweetness of the apple mixed with cinnamon, nutmeg, and a generous amount of butter. All light and fluffy and delicious.

"Did you both have good weekends?" Rodney asked.

Imani shook her head. "You haven't heard?"

"My wife and I were out of town until late last night," Rodney said. "Did something happen?"

"Yes, something awful." I slid a tea bag into my cup and explained about Darcy's death.

Both Rodney and Imani were shocked that I had found the body and filled with sympathy for Darcy's family.

"There is one tiny bit of good news," I added as I sat down with my tea.

"Oh?" Imani looked hopeful.

"I saw Harry Myers this morning. The police think they've figured out the killer, and that the murder had nothing to do with the festival. It can still go ahead."

"Well, that's positive, I guess," Imani said.

"You guess?" Rodney broke off a chunk of muffin and popped it in his mouth. "Having the killer arrested is the best thing that can happen at this point—for everyone's safety and for the festival. You know the community needs the Dogwood Festival. It draws us all together, and the money we raise goes to a good cause."

Imani twisted her hands together. "I know, and I support the festival in general. It's just that, for Dale and me, I'm afraid this year is going to be a disappointment."

"Why?" I would have thought, since Imani's husband was a local woodworker, that the festival would be a very profitable time for them. Over one weekend, Dale would probably sell hundreds of chopping boards, bowls, and kitchen utensils. His pieces were gorgeous.

"Normally, the festival is fantastic for Dale's business,"

Imani said. "And this year, we have things all arranged so my mom will watch the baby and we can both be at the festival. If I'm not helping at the tent for the museum, I'll be in the woodworking tent."

"That all sounds smart," I said. "I'm glad your mom can help out. So why do you think it will be a disappointment? From what I've heard, we might have a record crowd this year."

"The problem," she said, "is that I don't think that crowd will ever find us. For years, even before we got married, Dale's had the same spot, right near the wine and beer garden. This year he's on the far east side of all the vendors, as far from the stage and the beer garden as possible, facing the portable restrooms."

"I'm sorry Dale got a less desirable spot," I said. Harry had warned the steering committee that some vendors might be upset. "Harry used a new system this year to place people in vendor spots randomly. He said it would be fairer."

Imani sighed. "It probably is fairer. But the festival is a lot more important to someone who runs a craft business year-round than to someone who has a full-time job with benefits and sells stuff one weekend a year for the fun of it."

True. I bit my lower lip. "Harry said the vendor locations can't be changed at this point." He had told us horror stories about a festival that switched their plans at the last minute. "All we can do is hope that Detective Harper wraps things up quickly and that our marketing will bring in so many extra people that all the vendors, even ones in less desirable locations like you, will have lots of shoppers."

"All the local hotels and B & Bs are booked," Rodney said. "Even reservations in nearby towns are difficult to come by."

"Well, that's good news." Imani took another bite of muffin.

I relaxed back in my chair. The festival was going to be okay. Yes, Darcy's death was a tragedy, but Detective Harper had the situation in hand and had told me to stay out of it.

I should focus on the good things, like the fact that my staff was amazing. The three of us worked so well together, each bringing our own talents and gifts. With luck, the festival would be a success. Tourists and local residents alike would enjoy the museum's tent, and the museum would bring in even more visitors, gain more members, and—

My phone dinged with a text from Cleo.

As I scanned it, my breath caught.

*I have to talk to you. That idiot Detective Harper arrested Bryce.*

I excused myself, dialed Cleo's number, and hurried up the back stairs to my office.

She answered on the first ring. "Oh, Libby, thank you for calling."

I unlocked my office door, opened the dark, wooden blinds, and dropped my purse behind my large, mahogany desk. "The police arrested Bryce?" I asked as I sat down.

"He looked totally in shock when he saw Darcy. And why would he kill his fiancée?"

"He and Darcy weren't engaged anymore," Cleo said. "Saturday night they had a huge fight, and he broke up with her for good."

Even a relative newcomer like me was familiar with the Darcy-Bryce relationship drama. "They break up and get back together as often as I change the head on my fancy electric toothbrush." My father, a dentist, gave me the latest model and a stash of new toothbrush heads every Christmas so I could switch them out every three months.

"Not this time. This was different. Darcy told a friend on Sunday morning that Bryce said they were never getting back together, and that she should find a new vet for her cat."

That did sound final. "And Detective Harper believes Bryce was so mad that he killed her? Why did they break up?"

"Nobody knows." Cleo shrugged.

"If they'd broken up, would he kill her?"

"Of course not!" Cleo exclaimed. "Detective Harper is clutching at straws. Probably trying to find a quick solution before the festival. Bryce would never in a million years kill someone. That's why I called you."

An uneasy tickle squirmed in my stomach. I knew what she was going to say next.

"You need to figure out who really did this, Libby. Because it's definitely not Bryce. He's a veterinarian, for heaven's sake. He takes care of injured animals. Does that sound like someone who would commit murder?"

"Well, no." The man I'd seen at the fairgrounds, who was so in shock when he saw the wound on Darcy's head that he was immobilized, didn't seem like a murderer.

I'd watched Detective Harper handle other cases. He did have a tendency to fixate on one suspect and ignore other possibilities. And my friends and I had succeeded in finding the real killer on more than one occasion.

But this attack on Darcy had been vicious, and Detective Harper's warning to me had been very clear. He wanted me to stay out of this investigation for my own safety.

"Libby." Cleo's voice sounded wobbly. "You'll solve this, won't you?"

The image of Darcy's bloody head swirled in my brain.

"Libby?"

If Bryce wasn't the murderer, that meant the killer was still out there. Plus, Darcy's family deserved justice. Oh, I'd always been someone who believed in following and upholding the rules, but after my ex-husband didn't—and finagled things so I lost my job back in Philadelphia—I held those beliefs in fairness even more strongly. And the last thing Dogwood Springs needed was some unsuspecting tourist murdered at the upcoming festival.

My breath leaked out, and I hadn't even realized I'd been holding it. I sat up straighter in my desk chair. "Yes, I'll try to solve it. But I'll need help from you and our friends."

"You know you've got it," Cleo said.

After another minute on the phone, I tried to get down to work. But for the rest of the day, even when I went home to take care of Bella at lunchtime, thoughts of Darcy's murder swirled through my mind.

My friends and I had solved murder cases in the past in Dogwood Springs. Hopefully, we could solve this one as well.

# Chapter Five

THAT EVENING, after I let Bella out and fed her, I watched *Antiques Roadshow* while eating a quick dinner of leftover tacos. Then I stepped into the front entryway of my house and called up the stairs to Cleo in her apartment. "Ready?"

"Ready!" She came down the slightly wonky old stairs faster than I would have, but then she lived on the second floor, so she used them every day. "Can everyone join us?"

"Everyone but Doug. Alice says he's out of town, meeting with suppliers for his business." I clipped on Bella's leash, and the three of us stepped outside.

Although she was about the same age as my mom, Alice VanMeter, the president of the museum board, was a good friend of mine. She had helped me solve several mysteries, but her husband, Doug, who ran an online gift-basket business, traveled a lot and had only been involved in one of our cases.

Cleo and I walked side by side, with Bella leading the way.

"Sam's back from California?" Cleo shifted the jacket she was carrying to the other arm.

"He got in last night." Sam Collins, the man I'd been seeing, taught computer science at Grove University but had previously run a very lucrative tech firm in California. So lucrative that, although someone might not guess it when they met him, his net worth was about half a billion dollars. He'd recently traveled back to the West Coast to check on something related to his former company.

"Glad he's back," Cleo said. "And I know Zeke will be there."

Zeke, Cleo's sixteen-year-old nephew, might have seemed an unlikely member of our group. But his keen mind had proven to be a real asset in previous cases, as had his connections with the younger people in town. Zeke was good at thinking outside the box, and he and Sam often used their tech knowledge to find clues the rest of us couldn't.

The café was even closer than the museum. By the time Cleo finished telling me about a time in high school when Bryce had cared for an injured rabbit until it was well enough to be released back into the wild—a story punctuated by her declarations that someone so tenderhearted could never be a murderer—we were stepping into the fenced-in outdoor seating area at the café.

The Dogwood Café was right in the heart of downtown. Almost every one of its green metal outdoor tables was full, with people chatting and enjoying supper. The big umbrellas were out but lowered since the sun was fading.

"Look," I said to Cleo, pointing. "Sam's already got our table." A warm tendril wrapped around my heart at the sight of him. Tall, with perpetually rumpled dark hair, dark eyes, and black, rectangular-framed glasses, he looked incredibly handsome in jeans and a dark blue St. Louis Cardinals' sweatshirt. I bent down to Bella. "Go to Sam, girl."

Bella led the way over but stopped twice on the way to allow people sitting at nearby tables to pet her.

By the time I'd adopted her, after her previous owner, a retired FBI agent, had passed away, Bella had already made friends with most people in town. With her outgoing personality, it was pretty much a given that if I took her out, she'd find an old friend or make a new one.

We joined Sam at our favorite table, the one at the edge of the seating area where there was a protected corner big enough for a golden retriever to lie down.

"Hey, Libby." Sam pulled me in for a quick kiss, then bent to scratch between Bella's ears and tell her what a good dog she was.

Bella wagged her tail and looked up at him with love. I knew, without a doubt, that I was Bella's favorite human, but since we'd been dating, Sam had moved into a close second.

He was pretty important to me as well. With his logical, curious mind and great sense of humor added to that sexy geek look, I was hooked. "Welcome back to Missouri," I said as I sat down next to him.

"Glad to be back. Although I'm sorry you had such a traumatic experience while I was gone. It had to be horrible finding Darcy's body."

"It was." A memory of the bloodied back of her head flashed through my mind again. "I didn't know her well, but no one should die like that."

Sam reached over and gave my hand a reassuring squeeze.

I gazed at him a moment, grateful to have such a supportive man in my life. Then I looked up and saw Alice and Zeke entering the outdoor seating area.

Alice not only served as the president of the museum board, but she was also the number one volunteer. One of the kindest people I knew, she helped at the museum every Monday, but I'd missed seeing her today because I had so many meetings. She must have been to Cleo's salon recently, because her chin-length, tousled brown hair was shorter than the last time I'd seen it. She wore a mossy green sweater and matching pants. As always, Alice looked confident and capable.

I hadn't seen Zeke in a few weeks, and he appeared to have grown an inch taller. Or maybe he was simply standing up straighter. Tall and lanky, he didn't always seem comfortable with his height. Today, as he often did, he wore jeans, a T-shirt, a black hoodie, and black Converse tennis shoes.

The two made their way through the crowded seating

area and joined us, both bending down to say hello to Bella, who left her cozy corner to greet them, and offering their sympathies that I'd found Darcy's body.

I thanked them and suggested we order quickly so we could get down to the business of trying to solve the murder.

I'd learned from experience that Zeke had a gift for picking the best dessert on the menu. When he ordered the coconut layer cake with lemon filling, along with a cherry Coke, I did the same, except I switched the drink to hot tea. Alice passed on dessert and asked only for decaf coffee. Sam had Dutch apple pie, and Cleo opted for a hot fudge sundae.

While the others ordered, I looked at each of them around the table. These were people I could trust and count on, whether I had a personal crisis or we were working together to solve a mystery.

As soon as the server left the table, I turned to Cleo. "Can you fill everyone in on Bryce's arrest?"

"Will do." She rested her hands on the table. "You all know I dated Bryce in high school, right?"

Everyone nodded.

"I can assure you," she said, speaking more quietly than she normally did, "there is no way he committed murder. No. Way." She paused for a moment as if to make sure her point had sunk in. "Detective Harper thinks Bryce killed Darcy because their relationship ended. But I know, from what she told a friend of hers, that he was the one who broke up with her. It doesn't even make sense that he'd kill her. She was the person who might have been angry, not him."

"Whoever killed Darcy had to be at the fairgrounds that afternoon," I said. "Most likely, with the way three sides of the grounds are bounded by the river, and the fourth by Hartley Road, it was probably someone who was parked in one of the two lots."

"After they widened it and took out most of the shoulder, nobody in their right mind would walk on the edge of the road," Cleo said.

"You wouldn't want to ride a bike on Hartley Road either," Zeke added. "Not with how fast people drive, no bike lane, and a ravine on one side."

And unlike in a city, there was no public transportation in Dogwood Springs.

"So who did you see there that day?" Alice asked me.

"I parked in the smaller lot near the stage." I looked around to be sure they knew where I meant.

Five heads bobbed up and down. Even Sam, who had only lived in town a couple of years, knew the fairgrounds.

"Besides my car, there were only two other vehicles in the stage lot. One was a dark blue SUV that I'd seen Darcy driving. It had a bumper sticker for Dogwood State Bank, so I'm almost certain it was hers. The other car was driven by a man named Cameron Sidwell. His stepdaughter, Noelle Carson, is one of the queen candidates." It had taken a while, but I'd finally remembered her last name.

"Cameron works at the same bank as Darcy did," Alice said. "And his aunt, Eileen Davidson, moved to town last year. She's the owner of the new barbecue place, the Pit & Pickle."

Interesting. I hadn't realized Cameron and the new restaurant owner were related. Luckily, I could always count on Cleo and Alice to know all the small-town connections.

The server arrived with our drinks and desserts, and we put our suspect speculations on hold for a moment or two. Sam shared what his dad, who lived in St. Louis, had said about the pitching in the Cardinals' game yesterday.

As soon as the server walked away, we resumed our conversation.

"I heard that Mr. Sidwell was really mad at the police for making him stay so long to be questioned." Zeke slid his plate closer. "He was worried about Noelle and made Detective Harper send a police officer to find her."

That matched with what I overheard. "But where was Noelle? Why didn't she come with her dad when I called for help?"

"She was having a big fight with Kayla, one of the other queen candidates, near the restrooms. Noelle says Kayla stole her boyfriend." Zeke rolled his eyes.

*Mm-hmm.* Apparently, high school was just as delightfully drama-filled these days in Dogwood Springs as it had been when I attended more than a decade ago back in Columbus, Ohio. I took a bite of my dessert. The delicate cake contrasted perfectly with the tangy lemon filling and the creamy coconut frosting. I sat for a moment, thankful both that I was no longer a teenager and that I'd ordered the same dessert as Zeke. Once again, he'd picked a winner.

"So that gives us three possible suspects who we know were at the park." Sam counted them off on his fingers. "Cameron, Noelle, and Kayla."

"From what I heard, Noelle and Kayla were too busy fighting to have killed Darcy," Zeke said.

Sam pulled out his phone. "I could see that. They were probably too focused on each other to kill someone else. I'll start my list with Cameron."

"I can tell you the other people I saw at the park," I said. "The festival director, Harry Myers, was with me when I found Darcy. And besides Bryce, a few other people came when I called for help. A park worker named Aaron Eckhart, plus Zoe Thompson and her mom, Madison."

"Zoe's no killer," Zeke said quickly. "If Cleo can vouch for Bryce, I can vouch for Zoe."

Cleo's eyes narrowed, as if she might be picking up on a deeper connection between Zeke and Zoe than he'd previously let on, that the two of them might be dating. "What about her mom?"

Zeke shrugged. "I don't really know Zoe's mom. They don't get along all that well, but that doesn't necessarily make her a killer."

"No, it doesn't." Alice cradled her coffee cup. "Zoe's what? Sixteen?"

"Fifteen," Zeke said. "She skipped a grade."

"That can be a hard time for mothers and daughters,"

Alice said. "And Libby, I think I know the Aaron you mean. Blond, kind of scruffy beard, maybe in his late twenties?"

"That sounds like him," I said.

"He's local and has worked for the parks department since he graduated high school," Alice said. "He also does landscaping on the weekends. A hard worker, from what I hear."

"I wish I knew who else might have been at the fairgrounds." I took another forkful of cake, making sure to get both lemon filling and coconut frosting.

Cleo gave me a superior smile. "Ask and you shall receive. I've got the scoop from Sue Ann, the police dispatcher. She's in the salon almost every week now that she's got acrylic nails."

"Go on." I made a hurry-up gesture.

"So, first of all, after the coroner had a chance to look at the body, he said it was definitely a murder. Something about where the wound was located."

"It was high on the back of her head." I touched my own head in the approximate spot. "I don't see how you could fall and hit your head in that spot unless you were falling down a flight of stairs."

"That's almost exactly how Sue Ann explained it. They think someone probably hit her with a rock and threw it in the waterfall," Cleo said. "Also, the police learned Darcy was downtown with a friend before she came to the fairgrounds. She couldn't have gotten to the fairgrounds until right before two thirty. So she was killed sometime between then and two forty-five, when you found her, Libby."

A chill ran through me. If Bella hadn't seen that toad and stopped, I might have run into the killer. "Did the police learn anything else?"

Cleo nodded. "Sue Ann said the only cars in the main lot when the police arrived were a truck with Aaron's landscaping logo on it, Bryce's truck from the vet clinic, Madison's SUV, and that fancy silver Mercedes that Harry drives. The one with three bumper stickers advertising the festival. From the statements the police took, it seems like no one saw any other vehicles." She took a quick sip of her soda. "Sue Ann even knew the order they'd arrived in—Aaron, Madison, then Harry, then Bryce."

The timing seemed off to me. "If Bryce was the last to arrive, how would he have had time to kill Darcy before Harry and I found her?"

"This is where it gets ridiculous." Cleo huffed out a breath. "Detective Harper has this stupid theory that Bryce was actually there earlier. Like, he killed Darcy, left to go change his clothes and wash off any blood, then came back to 'help' when her body was discovered."

"That isn't stupid. It would give Bryce a good excuse if he left any trace evidence at the scene," Sam said.

Cleo glared at him. "As I said, a stupid theory."

Sam wasn't phased in the least by her comment. "We've avoided a key question. Bryce isn't on the festival steering committee, is he, Libby?"

I shook my head.

"Then why was he at the fairgrounds?" Sam raised both

eyebrows. "It seems like he was probably there to see Darcy."

*Hmm. Good point.*

Cleo looked down, and her face disappeared behind her long bangs.

"So," Sam said. "If, to be thorough, we include both Bryce and Zoe, we've got six suspects: Cameron, Harry, Zoe, Madison, Bryce, and Aaron."

Cleo held up a hand. "Wait. There's one other person who would have had access to the area."

"Who?" I asked.

"Okay, I know this sounds far-fetched, but I have this vague memory that Sylvia Snodgrass's land is on the other side of the river at the back of the fairgrounds. Her driveway is on Little Oaks Road, which runs parallel to Hartley Road, but farther north."

I pictured the Dogwood River. "So she swam across, killed Darcy, and swam back?" The idea seemed crazy on so many levels, mainly because Harry had said the water was freezing.

"No. I'd imagine she had a kayak and paddled across and back."

"Okay..." I tried to keep the disbelief out of my voice. "Three questions. One, does she have a kayak? Two, how would she know where Darcy was going to be? And three, why would Sylvia want to kill her?"

"If my land fronted the river, I'd have a kayak," Cleo said. "Anyone who talked to one of the queen candidate finalists would know when the photo shoot would be, and the photo has been taken by the waterfall for years." Cleo hesitated. "But I don't have a motive for Sylvia." She sighed. "Of course, at this point, we don't have a motive for most of our suspects."

"That's true," Alice said.

Zeke wrinkled his nose. "Aren't kayaks bright colors? Wouldn't someone have noticed her on the river?"

"Not fishing kayaks," Cleo said. "They're often dark green."

"Okay." I did my best to hide my skepticism. "We can include Sylvia as a suspect. If we can talk to him, though, the logical place to start is with Bryce." I held up a hand to stop Cleo before she jumped down my throat. "He's got the most to gain by helping us. And, as Darcy's former fiancé, he might know why someone wanted to kill her."

Gratitude flickered in Cleo's eyes, and she nodded.

"So that's where we should begin. If Bryce isn't the killer"—I looked at Cleo—"and I strongly doubt he is, then the murderer is still at large. For all we know, they might kill again. And that's the last thing anyone wants."

## Chapter Six

THAT NIGHT, as soon as we got home, Cleo went upstairs to text Bryce, and I took Bella out to the backyard.

An hour later, I'd already put on my pajamas and was in the kitchen preparing a few things to pack for lunch the next day when Cleo came thudding down the stairs.

"Libby?" she called through the door.

"C'mon in." I dug into the refrigerator, pulled out a bowl of grapes, and found a plastic container in the cabinet. "I'm in here."

Cleo walked into the kitchen and leaned against the counter. "Bryce is out on bail. If we go by his clinic tomorrow at seven thirty, before it opens, we can talk to him."

"Seven thirty?" Normally, I went to work at nine, and Cleo opened her salon at ten. I wasn't that excited about getting up extra early.

"He says he'll be swamped all day tomorrow. He missed today, thanks to the police."

"Okay." I glanced down at Bella. "We can talk to him, and then I'll run home to let Bella out again before I go to the museum."

"Great." Cleo walked toward the door. "I'll see you early tomorrow morning."

She went back upstairs, and Bella and I settled in for the night. Tomorrow, we'd begin our sleuthing in earnest.

The next morning, Bella woke me before my alarm. At some point in the night, I'd rolled onto my side with one hand stretched out over the edge of the bed. A cold, wet nose nudged my hand repeatedly until I surfaced into consciousness.

"I'm sorry, Bella," I said as I sat up. "I can't take you for a walk this morning, just a quick trip outside. Cleo and I have to go see Dr. Parker at the vet's office."

When Bella went to the vet, she saw Bryce's partner, Susie Parsons. But Bella had met Bryce there as well as once when he came by the house trick-or-treating with his niece.

As I climbed out of bed, I noticed the rain pouring outside. According to the weather app on my phone, it was going to rain hard all day. That meant no long walk for Bella in the evening either, just a whole day alone in my apartment.

"How about you come with me to the vet?" I offered. "A ride in the car?"

When I'd first adopted her, one way I'd recognized Bella's intelligence was by noticing how many words she knew. I wasn't totally sure she understood the word "vet," but she definitely understood "car." She let out a happy bark.

Twenty minutes later, I pulled into the parking lot at the Dogwood Springs Veterinary Clinic with Bella and Cleo in my car. Bella had been reluctant to let Cleo have the front passenger seat. She'd made up for it by riding in the back with her head between the two of us, eagerly watching out the windshield.

I let Bella out, clipped on her leash, and tried to keep both of us covered with my umbrella. Cleo knocked, but no one came to the door of the low brick building. She walked in, calling out to Bryce.

I followed, wiped my feet on the mat, and propped my umbrella by the door.

Bella let out a loud bark, nose a-quiver.

A handsome brown tabby with big, greenish-gold eyes sat on the high counter, peering down at Bella. The cat showed no fear as if it knew it was perfectly safe.

And in charge of the entire clinic.

The place was quiet, plainly furnished with blue plastic chairs and easy-to-clean linoleum, and smelled of strong disinfectant. There was no sign of Bryce, but after a moment, we heard a faint barking and then footsteps.

"Sorry I didn't get here more quickly." Bryce emerged from the side hall. His lab coat was freshly pressed, but his face seemed slightly gray as if he were exhausted. "I was in the back, checking on a dog that's recovering from surgery." He knelt down to talk to Bella eye to eye, then stood up and rubbed the cat's cheek. "I see you've met our latest staff member."

"Staff member?" Cleo said.

"This is Dr. Whiskers." Bryce continued petting the cat, and I heard loud, rumbly purring.

"He sees all patients when they first check in, of course, but his primary duty is maintaining staff morale." Bryce cleared his throat. "Particularly important when one of the vets has been arrested."

"Which was absolutely ridiculous." Cleo rolled her eyes. "I have no idea how Detective Harper could believe you might be a murderer."

"Thanks." He glanced down, then gestured to chairs in the waiting room. "I really appreciate that you believe in me." The three of us sat. "Do you think you can help?"

"We're certainly willing to try if you'd like," I said. "Please tell us what you know."

"Thanks. My lawyer got me out on bail, but he says the police consider the case practically closed." He stared down at his hands.

My stomach sank. That didn't sound good. And it didn't match the expression I'd seen on Bryce's face when he saw Darcy's body. Or Cleo's trust in him. "Let's start with the obvious. Why were you at the fairgrounds on Sunday?"

Bryce rested his hands on his thighs. "Saturday night, Darcy and I broke up. For good. It wasn't an easy situation, but after four phone calls the next morning, she finally believed me when I said we weren't getting back together. She came by to get some of her stuff and accidentally left her phone in my kitchen. I had to drive into town to check on some of my patients, and I knew she'd be doing the photo shoot. I thought it would be easier to drop off her phone at the fairgrounds than for her to come back to the house and get involved in another long discussion."

I could understand that. "Ordinarily, it would be none of my business, but, given the circumstances, I have to ask. Why, exactly, did you break up with her? You two have been together for a long time."

He shifted in his seat. "I, uh, I feel bad about that. Maybe if I'd been more, I don't know, self-aware, I might have realized we weren't meant to be married." He glanced at Cleo. "It was a lot of things, but remember my cousin from up in Jefferson City who has the same birthday as me? The kid we called Moose?"

Cleo nodded.

"I saw him and his wife recently. After watching the two of them together, I finally realized that Darcy and I would never have that type of relationship, and that was what I wanted." Bryce rubbed a thumb along a wrinkle in his jeans. "If I'd known she was going to die the next day, I never would have broken up with her. I hate that she was so unhappy the last few hours she was alive." His voice trailed off at the end, filled with emotion.

He might not have wanted to marry Darcy, but he was taking her death hard.

Bella's nails clicked against the tile floor as she walked close to Bryce. She nudged his knee and rested her head on his thigh.

His shoulders lifted. He petted her head and murmured something to her that I couldn't understand.

Outside, there was a bright flash of lightning, and thunder cracked.

Somewhere in the back of the clinic, several dogs began barking. Although her ears twitched, Bella remained silent and supportive by Bryce's side.

"But why does the detective think you killed her?" Cleo asked.

"I have no idea. I'd already broken up with her. I didn't need to kill her to know she would no longer be a part of my life."

Okay, but if he didn't commit the crime, someone else had. "You knew Darcy better than anyone. Was there anything going on in her life, maybe something at the bank, that might have led to her death? Anyone who might have had a reason to kill her?"

"I don't know much about the bank," Bryce said. "She was very careful about confidentiality, completely by the book with anything that had to do with money. But she did have an argument with someone recently."

Cleo and I both leaned in. "Who?" Cleo said.

"That new guy who's running the festival, Harry. I don't

know what it was about, but she was furious afterward," Bryce said.

"Harry?" I frowned. It seemed like he got along great with everyone, but maybe there was something I'd missed. Maybe all that charm was fake. "Did you tell the police?" I asked.

"I did." Bryce rubbed his hand along the wrinkle in his jeans again. "I don't know how much they believed me. It felt like Detective Harper thought I was trying to shove suspicion off on someone else."

"All you were doing was trying to help him find the real killer," Cleo said quickly.

I bit my lip. I wasn't a hundred percent sure of Bryce's innocence, like my friend. But hopefully, Detective Harper was following up on all leads, and if he wasn't, someone else needed to. "I don't know of any issues with the festival, but that doesn't mean there wasn't something going on. We'll talk to Harry."

"Thank you." Bryce gave Bella another pat. "I hope you can find something," he added, in a tone that sounded as if he didn't expect us to. "I'd better get to work. The rest of the staff should be here any minute, and I have a young schnauzer I should check on before today's patients arrive." He stood, and Cleo and I walked toward the door.

Bella cocked her head at Dr. Whiskers and gave a half-hearted bark.

Dr. Whiskers licked one paw and washed his face, without even a glance in Bella's direction.

"C'mon, Bella." I grabbed my umbrella and tugged at her leash. "Time to ride in the car again."

Head high, as if drawing attention to the fact that she, and not Dr. Whiskers, got to go in the car with me, Bella led Cleo and me out into the rain.

## Chapter Seven

I TOOK BELLA HOME, got her settled for the day, and had just enough time to text Alice to make plans for us to talk to Harry before I drove to work in the pouring rain.

For once, things at the museum were crisis free. Despite the deluge, all the volunteers showed up for their shifts. The number of morning visitors was encouraging, especially for a rainy Tuesday. And the building hadn't developed any maintenance issues overnight, which—no matter how hard we tried to stay on top of things—was always a possibility with a place that was more than a hundred years old.

The only flaw in my workday so far was the appearance of a large, creepy-looking spider near the ceiling in my office. I tried to like spiders, as I knew almost all of them were good creatures that ate other bugs, but they still made me shudder. I kept imagining this one peering down at me, waiting to rappel down on a silken thread and leap onto my shoulder. I was ready to flick it down and smash it with my shoe when Imani intervened and carried it outside.

Once she returned, we spent the rest of the morning planning programming for the fall. We came up with some wonderful ideas for a series on the ways that waves of immigrants had affected the area. I volunteered to kick off the series with a presentation on the German immigrants who began arriving in the 1820s. They were best known for their passionate antislavery position during the Civil War, as well as the wineries and breweries they established. Although Dogwood Springs was not part of the Missouri German Heritage Corridor located farther north along the Missouri River, the influence of these immigrants on the state was too significant to ignore.

Just before twelve, Imani headed back to her office, and my phone dinged with a text from Alice.

*I'm in the parking lot. Come on out when you're ready to go see Harry.*

Excellent! Right on time. I'd take my lunch hour to talk to Harry, microwave my frozen burrito when I got back, and eat it and my grapes and cookies while I answered emails.

I grabbed my umbrella and big purse, hurried down the back stairs, and avoided as many puddles in the parking lot as I could while I made my way to Alice's white Lincoln SUV.

"How was Bryce when you and Cleo talked with him this morning?" she asked as I climbed in.

"He seemed okay." I folded my umbrella and tucked it behind my feet. "I guess having patients that need him helps a bit. He didn't actually accuse Harry of being the murderer, but it did seem like a lead we should follow up on."

"I already called in a carry-out order for myself to the Pit & Pickle," Alice said. "To give us a reason to be there."

"Great. I think Harry eats lunch there every day and then uses his table as a makeshift office for the festival steering committee all afternoon. Hopefully, we'll find him there before any committee members stop by to talk to him."

"On our way." Alice started the engine.

The Pit & Pickle Barbecue Joint, which only opened a month ago, was located close to Interstate 44, near the university exit—an ideal location for maximum traffic. Sam and I had talked about trying the place, but, since he had been out of town, we hadn't made it in yet.

Outside, the restaurant was nothing fancy. Just a one-story concrete block building with a new neon sign as its only decoration, but the parking lot was packed. Alice found a spot in the very back of the gravel lot, and the two of us walked in, sharing her enormous golf umbrella and discussing what we'd ask Harry.

As we walked in, Alice waved and called hello to a woman named Eileen, who was making the rounds of the dining room, greeting customers and thanking them for their business.

Eileen gave Alice a broad smile and held up a forefinger to indicate she'd be right over.

I looked around the Pit & Pickle.

In its previous life, the restaurant had served Chinese food and been a mash-up of 1970s' paneled walls and modern tables and chairs. Eileen had hung vintage soft-drink signs and replaced the furnishings with Formica tables and black vinyl diner-style booths. Almost every booth was taken, and a loud buzz of conversation filled the air, along with country hits from the 1980s. I spotted several people I knew, including Dallas McAllister, the wife of Sam's department chair, and Alan Melkins, a retired English professor who lived on my street.

I could see why Harry liked it here. The smell of slow-cooked meat, sweet and spicy sauce, and deep-fried onion rings was nearly intoxicating. A glass case by the register displayed plates of enormous chocolate chip cookies, gooey brownies, and individual pecan pies.

Lucky for us, Harry sat alone, nibbling an onion ring and reading on his phone.

I nudged Alice. "There he is. In that table near the back."

"Excellent," she whispered. "I'll introduce you to Eileen, and then we can talk to Harry."

"Alice." Eileen beamed as she walked up to us. "How lovely to see you." A note of genuine pleasure rang in her voice, and she gave off the vibe of someone really comfortable in her own skin. If I had to guess, I'd say she was older than Alice. Early sixties, maybe. She had shoulder-length, blondish-gray hair, brown eyes, and a tiny gap between her two front teeth.

Alice introduced me, mentioning my connection to the

museum. I invited Eileen to stop by and told her the food smelled fantastic.

"So nice to meet you, Libby." She gave me a kind smile. Then her eyes darted away to a slender, angry-looking blond woman who had just walked in. "Oh, please excuse me. That's my nephew's wife, Tiffany. She needs to speak with me." Eileen hurried off.

I angled my head toward the angry woman. "So she's married to Cameron, who works at the bank?"

Alice nodded.

Tiffany wore a lot more bling than I pictured for a conservative banker's wife, but maybe I was stereotyping her too much. Besides, I needed to focus on Harry.

Alice and I made our way across the room and stopped near his table.

He looked up. "Libby, Alice, how nice to see you. Are you here for lunch?"

"We're picking up a carry-out order," Alice said.

"I'm glad I spotted you, Harry." I adjusted my purse strap, which was sliding down my shoulder. "I had a question about the festival. Maybe, while we wait…"

"Please, join me." Harry stood and gestured to the empty seats at the table, and Alice and I sat down.

As always, Harry presented the image of a wealthy man at leisure. He wore a burgundy polo from another golf course with an expensive pair of sunglasses hooked in the placket, dark gray track pants, a matching jacket with a gold zipper pull shaped like the "B" of an upscale brand, and what looked like brand-new tennis shoes.

"I heard that in addition to the murder, there was another problem with the festival," I said. "I was wondering if there was anything I could do to help."

"Well, as you might expect with a volunteer operation this big, there's a new problem every day." Harry gave a halfway shrug and turned up his palms as if resigned to dealing with human nature. "The latest was that the other barbecue place in town, which I was told has had the only barbecue stand at the festival for years, was all up in arms because the Pit & Pickle planned to have its food truck there."

*Hmmm.* Not the problem I'd meant, but I could see how the Pit & Pickle's popularity might make a dent in the business of the other barbecue restaurant—both at the festival and on a daily basis.

Harry gestured toward the register. "Do you know Eileen, the owner here?"

"I just met her."

"She's a good egg. She understands the festival is meant to draw the community together to work toward a common fundraising goal. She came to me, said she'd heard the other barbecue joint was upset, and offered to serve funnel cakes instead."

"Oh, that's wonderful. I'd been wondering who would handle funnel cakes," Alice said. She turned to me. "The couple that used to make them moved out of town."

"That was really generous of Eileen." I didn't know for sure, but I'd bet serving barbecue at the festival would be better advertising for the Pit & Pickle.

I vowed to come back here soon to give her my business in appreciation for her willingness to be so flexible in helping the festival. "And I do love funnel cakes." In my opinion, funnel cake was the festival food equivalent of a shortbread cookie. Granted, funnel cake was greasier, but from what I'd seen, grease seemed to be a key ingredient in fair and festival foods.

"I'm glad you like them," Harry said. "Eileen's going to park her food truck right next to the museum tent."

"Excellent." I beamed at Alice. "If her funnel cakes smell as good as her barbecue, people will flock to her food truck. While they're waiting in line, we can tell them about the museum." I turned back to Harry. "Actually, the issue I heard about involved the queen contest. Was that anything I could help with?"

"Darcy's death was a tragedy. She was so young." He shook his head. "I don't want to make a big deal over it with her gone, but I guess I can tell you. Recently, I was concerned that Darcy had been unfair in eliminating Zoe Thompson from the queen contest. From what I saw in the interviews, it seemed like Zoe should have moved on to the finals. And her mother had indicated how important the contest was to Zoe."

Alice nodded. "I can see how that would be concerning. The contest has to be fair."

"That was my thinking as well, but Darcy got quite defensive when I spoke with her. She said I had no right to question her integrity, and that she had chosen the finalists appropriately. I finally decided I had to trust her. I don't believe in micromanaging. But she sure acted prickly about the whole thing."

From what I'd observed, Darcy could be charming when she wanted. When she didn't make the effort, though, "prickly" was a good way to describe her. "I wonder if that prickliness, as you put it, is what got her killed. I, for one, don't believe Bryce killed her. But I don't know who else might have."

Harry sat back against the booth and rubbed a napkin over his mouth. "I don't want to spread rumors, but I did have one thought..."

I leaned in, hoping to encourage him.

"Well, you know I've worked with a couple of other festivals before, right?"

I did because he'd mentioned it at one of the steering committee meetings. Alice, though, looked intrigued, as if she wanted to hear the details.

"After my wife died, I wasn't sure where I wanted to spend my retirement. I knew I needed someplace different to help me move past the grief." He glanced away for a second and his Adam's apple rose and fell. "So I lived in three different places in three years. I'd helped with a town carnival where my wife and I lived and enjoyed it, so each time I moved, I got involved in something similar."

"That sounds smart," Alice said. "A good way to keep busy and help the community."

"Thank you, Alice. You're very kind." Harry took a sip of his coffee. "I know it sounds over the top, but I have seen a lot of drama related to queen contests. And if you remember, when we found Darcy's body, Zoe was there with her mom. I keep wondering why she was at the fairgrounds that day, and if, maybe she was so upset about being cut from the contest that..." He made an awkward gesture with his hands, too polite to say out loud that Zoe might have been Darcy's killer.

I glanced over at Alice. Zeke never talked much about his social life, but he'd let slip a comment from time to time that made it seem like he and Zoe spent a lot of time together. He'd also been quick to defend her when I mentioned she'd been at the park.

What if he was wrong? It was possible Zoe and her mom had gone there to talk to Darcy, to see if there might have been a mistake when she calculated the scores of the finalists. If Darcy had said no, things could have disintegrated from there.

Nope. I couldn't see it. Oh, I knew emotions ran high in teenagers. I remembered all too well how things I wouldn't consider a big deal now had gotten blown out of proportion in my mind back then. I hadn't had enough life experience to put them into perspective.

But still, the Dogwood Queen contest didn't seem like an honor that Zoe—or her mom—would find worth killing over.

The loudspeaker hummed to life. "Order for Alice," the person called.

"I guess we'd better go, Harry," Alice said. "We'll talk with Zoe, just to put your mind at ease." She looked at me, one eyebrow raised.

I nodded. We'd gotten all the information we could out of Harry. Despite my earlier doubts, he seemed genuinely nice. He'd explained the argument Bryce mentioned, and—although I thought it was unlikely—he'd given us a new lead.

Alice and I stood, and Harry, ever the gentleman, got to his feet as we left.

## Chapter Eight

"WHAT DO YOU THINK?" I asked Alice once we were back in her car.

She turned and put her carry-out bag and big umbrella below the back seat. "I don't know, Libby. On TV, the killer is often the husband. Bryce was as close to a husband as Darcy had. He seems a lot more likely of a suspect than a crazed teenage girl."

"Or her mother." I unzipped my light jacket, sending rivulets of water onto my dress pants and the leather seat of Alice's car. I brushed them off onto the floor. "It's going to be really hard on Cleo if Bryce is the murderer."

"I know." Alice started the engine and threaded her way out of the gravel parking lot. Without the painted lines of a paved lot, people had gotten rather creative about wedging in their cars.

"We should talk with Zoe and Madison. If nothing else, they were there that day. One of them might have seen something." I dug out my phone, which had sunk to the very bottom of my big purse. "I'll text Zeke and see if he can go with me. Maybe Zoe will be more willing to talk if he's there."

"Good idea," Alice said.

I sent the text, and a few minutes later, Alice dropped me by my car in the museum parking lot. Whatever sleuthing I did next would have to wait. First, I needed to dash home to let Bella out, and then get back to work.

At four o'clock, I emailed myself a draft of a letter I was writing to potential donors. I didn't like to shortchange the museum of my time, so after dinner, I planned to spend an hour or so polishing up the letter to get it ready to send.

In the meantime, according to Zeke, Zoe had color-guard tryouts all evening. If I wanted a chance to talk with her and her mom first, I needed to return to the Dogwood Springs Veterinary Clinic. Zoe worked there part-time after school, feeding the animals that were recovering from surgery and cleaning their pens.

I quickly packed up and drove across town to the vet's office. Inside, I added my soggy umbrella to a line by the door and walked up to the counter. I wasn't sure whether there had been an emergency cleanup, or if it was the effect of wet footprints on the floor, but the smell of disinfectant was stronger than it had been in the morning.

Zoe was nowhere to be seen, but her mom was busy

with a customer, explaining the benefits of the different types of prescription dog food the clinic sold.

I waited at the other end of the counter. After I'd been there a moment, Dr. Whiskers leapt from the floor behind the counter to the desktop and then to the high counter. He strolled along the counter, and—even though my clothes probably smelled faintly of dog—came right up to me.

"Hello." I held out my fingers to let him sniff them.

He nuzzled his head against my hand and began to purr loudly.

"Aren't you a sweetie?" I scratched between his ears and, when he angled his head, I obligingly rubbed under his chin. His fur was thick and plush, and he purred even louder. What a charmer.

"Libby?" Madison had finished with the customer and walked toward me. "Zeke and Zoe are already in the break room. Let's go on back."

"Certainly." I gave Dr. Whiskers a final pat.

Madison called to a woman in a back office, who came out to cover the front desk. A minute later, we joined Zeke and Zoe, who sat close together at a round table in the small break room. Now that I saw mother and daughter together again, their similarities seemed more pronounced. Narrow faces, the same shaped noses, and even the same taste in earrings—long, gold, and dangly, although Madison's looked like tassels and Zoe's had little gold stars on tiny chains.

Zeke leaned his head toward Zoe. "No reason to be

nervous. Just tell Libby what you told me. She'll believe you."

Normally, Zeke came across as quiet, and I'd imagined him as kind of a loner at school, but he and Zoe seemed very connected.

"I didn't intend to make you nervous, Zoe." I smiled across the table at her. "I was hoping you and your mom could tell me why you were at the fairgrounds on Sunday, and if you saw anything suspicious."

Madison smiled encouragingly at her daughter.

Zoe stiffened. Although I thought her mom should be present, I wondered if this conversation might be better without her. It hadn't been that long since I'd been in high school. Not so long that I couldn't recognize tension between a mom and a teenage daughter.

"That's simple," Madison answered for Zoe. "Kayla didn't have a ride because both her parents work on Sundays. I drove her to the fairgrounds so she could be in the photo. Zoe and I were just going to drop her off and then her dad could pick her up afterward, but she spilled Pepsi on her white blouse. You know how they were all supposed to wear jeans and white dress shirts for the picture?"

"I do." It had been my idea.

"Mom and I went with her to the indoor bathroom at the fairgrounds and tried to help her wash it out," Zoe said.

"We got out most of it," Madison said. "Because it hadn't had time to set. And we were in the restroom forever, drying it under the hand dryer."

"It still had kind of a shadow of the soda," Zoe added. "But we didn't think it would show in the photo." She drew a lock of her long curly red hair in front of her and ran one hand down it, then the other, her movements so jerky that I realized she was even more nervous than I'd thought. "When Kayla was all dressed again, and we came out, Noelle was there. Right away, they started fighting about who should be dating Cody, this guy on the football team."

"That's when we heard you calling for help," Madison said. "So Zoe and I left them there, squabbling, and ran toward where we thought your voice was coming from."

"And then we ... we saw Darcy." Zoe pressed her lips together.

"So they were with Kayla. Neither of them would have had time to kill Darcy." Zeke crossed his arms over his chest and glared at me.

"Or a reason," Madison said.

"What about the fact that you didn't make the list of finalists yourself?" I asked Zoe.

"I was disappointed," Madison cut in.

"But I wasn't that upset." Zoe exchanged glances with Zeke. "The queen contest is more of a cheerleader-volley-ball-girl kind of thing."

"As for the scholarship money she might have won if she'd been named queen, honestly, Libby, $5,000 would be wonderful, but Zoe would be better off putting the time into her studies than spending it on all the stuff the queen has to do. Maybe she's too modest to tell you, but she's so bright that she's likely to get a lot more money than that if she does well in her classes."

I looked over at Zeke.

He nodded.

"Besides," Zoe said, "I kind of admired Darcy. She always dressed so cute, and I guess I respected her because I knew she had to be good at math to do her job."

"And I certainly didn't want Darcy dead." Madison raised a hand to her heart. "We've been friends since high school."

I hadn't thought about it earlier, but Madison and Darcy were probably close to the same age.

"But I work with Bryce. I don't believe he killed her either," Madison added quickly.

"No way," Zoe said.

At this point, Zeke shot me a pointed glance, as if I should have realized by now that questioning Zoe as a suspect was a waste of time.

He was right. But maybe she or her mom had seen something—anything—that could be helpful. "Do you have any idea who might have done it? Or anything suspicious you noticed that day?"

Zoe and Madison both shook their heads, and their gold, dangly earrings bounced back and forth.

"Sorry," Madison said. "I'd like to help. I wish we had some clue to offer you."

I thanked them and Zeke, stopped to give Dr. Whiskers some more attention on my way out, and made my way through the rain to my car.

Once I shut the car door, I slumped in my seat as I ran through the investigation so far. We'd talked to Bryce. We'd followed up his suggestion and talked to Harry. Then we'd followed up on Harry's suggestion and talked to Zoe and her mother.

And I still had absolutely no idea who the killer could be.

## Chapter Nine

FOR HOURS, ever since Alice and I had visited the Pit &
Pickle at lunch, the delicious mix of aromas in the restaurant had lingered in my mind. Was it any wonder that,
when Sam asked where I wanted to eat dinner, I picked the
new barbecue place?

He arrived at my house at seven, right on time. When he
kissed me hello, Bella wriggled between us, eager to be
noticed. Sam bent down to rub her tummy, and while he
discussed with her how unfortunate it was that it had
rained all day, I secretly admired how handsome he looked
in jeans and a dress shirt. Then he and I went out to his
blue Tesla.

"I got the text you sent everyone," he said as he started
down Elm. "Tell me more about Zoe and Madison. Did you
have other thoughts, perhaps something you didn't want to
say to Zeke?"

"Just that Zoe seemed awfully nervous while we were talking."

"Well, she is only fifteen. And she saw Darcy's body, too, right?"

"She did. Which was bad enough for me, an adult who's come across other murder victims." I settled back into the car seat. "I bet you're right. Probably talking with me reminded her of seeing the body and stressed her out. She seems like a sweet girl, and I don't think she had anything to do with Darcy's death. I just wish we were making progress more quickly on finding the killer."

"This has happened when we've worked on mysteries before." Sam rested his hands atop the steering wheel at a stop sign. "You feel like you're stuck, and then you suddenly find a clue that really helps."

"True." That didn't mean I enjoyed feeling stymied.

"Have you heard any news about our historical mystery?" he asked.

"Not a word. I haven't had a single positive response to the social media post I asked my friends who work in other museums to share about Ivy."

When Sam bought his house, Ashlington, a place that had been built by my ancestors long ago, he'd found a mysterious painting in the attic. Initially, it looked like the work of the famous American artist Clayton Smithton, but some of the details didn't fit the time period. Thanks to an art restorer, we learned that the famous artist had painted a family of four in the portrait: a mother, a father, and two girls. Years later, an unknown artist added more background to the portrait, painting over one of the girls.

Intrigued, we'd done some historical sleuthing. We identified the girl who had been removed from the painting as Ivy Anne Whitfield, born in 1887. We learned she left Dogwood Springs, then called Silersville, in 1905, to escape a marriage being forced on her by her father and stepmother. Even more interesting, we discovered that, after Ivy left town, her parents faked her death in order to profit from it. We even found letters she wrote to a friend in town that mentioned she'd married a dairy farmer, but they were signed only with a drawing of a single ivy leaf and gave no return address.

Despite using every historical research method I knew, we hadn't learned any further details of what had happened to her. Finally, I'd shared her image on social media, thinking someone might have seen a photo of her in later life and recognized the young woman with brown hair and big dark eyes. But we hadn't had any more luck with that mystery than we had with figuring out who killed Darcy.

Because of the rain, Sam dropped me at the door of the Pit & Pickle. Thankfully, once I walked into the restaurant, my sleuthing frustrations melted away—helped in large part by the heaping plate of glistening golden onion rings that passed by on a server's tray. They smelled so delicious that it was hard to focus on anything now but dinner.

I waved at Eileen as she bustled by, and then I put our name on the list. Despite the dozen people crowded near the hostess stand, we only had an expected wait of five to ten minutes. I found a seat at an empty booth near the door and fought back a chuckle when I saw Harry sitting on the other side of the waiting area. If the Pit & Pickle was so good that he wanted to eat here twice in one day, Sam and I were bound to enjoy our dinner.

The loudspeaker announced a pickup order for Jack, and Harry got up and went to the register. A moment later, he stepped back, looking flustered. "It's a bit loud in here," he muttered to himself. He shrugged and waved a hand to one side as if to brush aside his embarrassment as he went back to his seat.

Indeed, it was hard to hear. Everyone in the waiting area seemed to be trying to talk louder than the people around them.

"I've got my own theory about Darcy's murder," I heard the gray-haired woman sitting next to me say to her companion.

All thoughts of dinner left my mind. I edged slightly closer to the conversation.

"Do tell." The second woman's eyes lit behind her red-framed glasses, and her voice held a note of delight as if she liked a juicy tidbit of gossip even better than barbecue.

I looked away, not wanting to appear to be eavesdropping, but hanging on every word.

"Well," the first woman said, "I think the killer was Sylvia Snodgrass."

"Really?" The eager gossiper sounded giddy.

The first woman lowered her voice, but I could still hear her plainly. "I heard Darcy was the main person who lobbied for Sylvia to be replaced as festival director when she got sick. It wasn't like Sylvia had anything life-threatening. She might have missed a couple of weeks, but she could have handled the festival, no problem. Darcy used Sylvia's illness as an excuse to suggest Harry as her replacement. And you know being in charge meant the world to Sylvia. She loved being the queen bee."

"Ooh, I bet you're right. Since she'd been in charge for so long, she would have known exactly where the photo of the queen candidates would be taken. And how to sneak off through the trees unnoticed."

"Libby?" Sam touched my shoulder. "I checked with the hostess. Most of these other people waiting are here with a large party, but they can seat us now."

Oops. I'd been so busy pretending not to eavesdrop that I hadn't even seen him come in. I grabbed my purse and stood, eager to share what I'd overheard.

A waitress came by almost as soon as the hostess had seated us, and Sam and I quickly ordered. Once she stepped away from the table, I filled him in on what I'd learned.

He used his index finger to push up the bridge of his glasses. "Isn't that interesting? Sylvia does have a motive for killing Darcy." He pulled out his phone. "Let me check something."

"What?"

"When I bought my house, I used the website of the

local tax assessor to see who owned the properties around Ashlington, and what they'd sold for. Most didn't have houses on them as nice as the one your ancestors built, but I could at least see the value of the land. I want to verify what Cleo said earlier, that Sylvia owns the property on the other side of the river from the fairgrounds."

"Good idea." I was so lucky to be dating Sam. Not just handsome and fun, but really smart.

The server appeared with our drinks, and I took a sip of my hot tea. "Any luck?" I asked Sam.

He drummed his fingers on the table. "The assessor's site is kind of slow."

I dug my own phone out of my purse. "While you're checking the ownership of the property, I'm going to look at it in satellite view. Cleo's kayak theory might not be viable, but if I see a path from the river to Sylvia's house…"

"Great idea." Sam tapped his phone again.

The app I opened was a lot faster than the assessor's site. It only took me a second before I saw the fairgrounds on the map. I zoomed in. Goosebumps shot up on my arms.

Sam leaned forward. "She owns it, Libby. The whole swath of land across the river behind the fairgrounds. Sylvia H. Snodgrass."

My breath caught. I handed my phone to Sam. "Look."

He set his phone on the table and picked up mine. "What am I looking at?"

"Not only is there what seems to be a path running to the river from the back of Sylvia's house, but there's also what looks like a small bridge." I pointed. "Right there, leading from the end of the path across the river."

Sam's head jerked up. "You're kidding."

"Nope." I grinned. "The bridge ends a little way upstream from the waterfall to the east in a heavily wooded area. So Sylvia had a motive like that woman said. She had means, like anyone else, because she could pick up a rock. And she had opportunity. She could walk through her back-yard, slip down the path through the woods, go over the bridge, and be back at her house before anyone knew she'd killed Darcy."

Sam stared at the image on my phone, then handed it back. "And you were worried that you weren't making any progress solving this crime. Talk about finding some great clues."

"I know." I spotted the server coming toward our table with a loaded tray and slid my phone back in my purse. "First thing tomorrow, I need to find a way to talk to Sylvia. I thought Cleo was grasping at straws, trying to find someone besides Bryce who might have committed the crime. But Sylvia's definitely a suspect now."

An hour later, after a meal of outstanding beef brisket, the best onion rings I'd ever eaten, and an amazing tart-sized pecan pie that Sam and I split, he drove us back to my apartment.

He and I let Bella out, played with her, and then snuggled up on the couch to watch a rather goofy movie that was half rom-com, half mystery. Bella brought over her favorite toy, a stuffed chicken, and lay on the floor beside the couch. Soon she was fast asleep, and Sam and I were fully absorbed in the movie.

When the hero and heroine had solved the mystery and realized that, despite their differences, they really did love each other, Sam clicked off the TV and frowned. "I'd better head home," he said as he stood. "I've got an early class to teach, and I haven't done any prep yet."

"Yeah, I've got work tomorrow, too. Plus, I want to see if Alice or Cleo knows Sylvia well enough to engineer a way for us to talk with her. I can't show up at the woman's door alone and ask her if she killed Darcy."

"Definitely not." Sam took my hand as we walked to my front door. "Please don't confront any of the suspects alone, Libby. I don't want anything bad to happen to you." He slowed and pulled me to face him, and his tone grew more serious. "You're too important to me."

A light, fizzy feeling filled my veins, and I was struck anew by how much I cared for him and enjoyed our time together. "You're important to me, too, Sam."

Probably more important than I cared to admit. If I let myself, I could imagine a future of eating every dinner together. A future of snuggling on a couch every evening together. And a future of finding a lifetime of clues together.

Just the thought of it made my heart beat faster. I stepped closer to Sam and slid my arms around his waist.

He ran his fingertips gently down my cheek. "Sweet dreams."

I opened my mouth to wish him the same, and he covered my lips with his own.

My heart pounded, and I nestled closer against him as he kissed me again and again and again. Warmth filled every cell of my body, until I felt powerless to think of anything but his lips and his body, pressed up against mine. The rest of the world fell away, and my senses were filled with Sam and Sam alone.

At last, he stepped back, and I stared at him, breathless.

"Good night, Libby," he said in a husky voice.

"Good night, Sam," I whispered.

I opened the door for him, followed him out into the entryway, and watched him walk toward where he'd parked his car along the street.

Then I closed the door and leaned my back against it, allowing the air to whoosh out of my lungs.

How could I not be crazy about a man who could kiss like that?

## Chapter Ten

THE NEXT MORNING, after Bella and I had both had breakfast and taken an extra-long walk—all the way down Elm to Eighteenth Street and back—I contacted Cleo and Alice. Alice said she knew Sylvia. By the time I unlocked the front door of the museum at ten for visitors, we had a plan in place to go speak with her. Although I'd driven to work in case I needed my car, Alice offered to pick me up at twelve forty-five. I'd take my official lunch hour late and eat earlier at my desk.

Cleo, who had to run home from the salon for something she'd forgotten, would let Bella out at midday. I'd miss seeing my sweet dog at lunchtime, but I had a video call with a potential donor at three and needed every minute to prepare, outside of the window when I'd talk with Sylvia. Bella would miss me, but Cleo would spend quality time with her. And with the festival starting in only two days, we had to find every clue we could to identify Darcy's killer.

I spent the morning preparing for my three o'clock meeting and mentally rehearsing what I would say to Sylvia.

At a quarter 'til one, Alice picked me up right on time. We headed north on Main Street, then turned east on Little Oaks Road.

Unlike Hartley Road, a major artery of Dogwood Springs, Little Oaks Road had only a few small housing developments and, farther from town, scattered single-family homes. The road rolled up and down hills and curved around rocky outcrops. I didn't see any "little" oaks, but the road was lined with full-grown oaks, plus rich green cedars, redbuds, and—even out here where they were planted by nature instead of townspeople—plenty of dogwoods. Unlike yesterday, the sky was clear, and the drive was lovely.

"Thanks so much for arranging this, Alice."

"No trouble at all. After what you and Sam learned last night, I agree that we should talk to Sylvia." She focused on the road as we rounded a tight curve. Once the road straightened, Alice glanced over at me. "I do have my doubts, though, about her being the murderer. She ran the festival for so many years, and the Good Neighbor Fund means a lot to her. I can't quite see her killing Darcy at the fairgrounds a few days before the festival. Even if she wasn't in charge, she still wouldn't want to do anything that might hurt attendance."

I caught my lower lip between my teeth and thought. "You may be right. I guess we'll just have to see."

We rounded another couple of curves, and Alice turned onto a long driveway that led to a tall, wood-stained house in a contemporary style. She parked near the garage.

When we got out of the car, a middle-aged woman with poofy dark hair and narrow, oval glasses walked around the side of the house. She folded a pair of gardening gloves and set them on a table on her front patio.

"Come around to the back porch." She brushed at some dirt on the knees of her jeans. "I've been weeding my garden, and this is too much mud for my living room."

She led us around back and opened the door to a large, comfortable screened porch. Two cushy, red-checked outdoor couches, a pair of navy metal rockers, and a large dining table and chairs filled a space half as big as my apartment. She held the door as Alice and I walked in and then introduced herself to me. "Please, sit anywhere."

A bird I couldn't identify repeated a soft, two-note song, and trees rustled in the wind, making the tranquility of the porch almost palpable.

Alice and I sat on the couch, and Sylvia pulled up a metal rocker. She grabbed a worn sweater from a nearby table and slipped it on.

I looked around the room, trying to match the casual decor and the woman's relaxed attitude with the persnickety management style I'd heard about. The only connection I saw was in the way the furniture was neatly aligned with the indoor-outdoor area rug and in Sylvia's brown eyes, which held the same look of intelligence and experience as the eyes of some of my high school teachers.

The look that stopped most students before they tried any funny business.

"How can I help you all today?" Sylvia rocked her chair gently back and forth.

I started out exactly as Alice and I had planned. "The police seem certain that Bryce Parker killed Darcy Jackson at the fairgrounds on Sunday. I happened to be there because I was supposed to help Darcy take a photo of the queen candidates by the waterfall. But I find it hard to believe Bryce was the killer."

Sylvia let out an unladylike snort. "Bryce Parker, a killer? Hardly. I was still teaching at the high school when he went through. I never had him in my classes, but I know he's no murderer."

"I agree. That's why I wanted to see if you might have seen something that day. I was told your land backs up to the river behind the fairgrounds."

"It does," Sylvia said, but she didn't elaborate.

Alice and I had agreed we should try to get as much information out of Sylvia as possible before we did anything to indicate we suspected her. Still, it took a good deal of willpower not to ask about the bridge right away.

"Did you know Darcy in high school as well?" Alice asked.

"Yes, I had her in class for two years." Sylvia paused the rocker. "I still don't know why Bryce started dating her. The two of them were not well-suited."

"Oh?" I leaned forward, hoping she'd say more.

"I've always thought unless something drastic happens

like a near-death experience or some such, that by the time a person is in high school, their personality is fully formed." Sylvia started rocking back and forth again. "Oh, some kids go wild in their late teens and early twenties, but once they fully grow up, they revert back to their core personality."

"That matches up with what I've observed as well," Alice said.

I thought about myself and nodded.

"In high school, Bryce was a decent kid. Honest and kind, and he must have already known he wanted to be a vet because he worked very hard in school. I've heard it's even more difficult to get into vet school than med school."

"And Darcy?" I asked.

"That girl could act nicely if it suited her purposes, but underneath, she was very selfish."

*Selfish.* The same word Cleo had used to describe Darcy.

Even if she'd been selfish, though, Darcy hadn't deserved to be murdered. Time to dig a little deeper.

"I'm on the festival steering committee," I said. "I heard Darcy encouraged people to replace you as festival director right away when you got ill."

"It wasn't only Darcy." A shadow passed through Sylvia's eyes. "I thought I'd been running things in a way that was best for the festival, but maybe I didn't communicate my reasons very well." She gave a wry smile. "Or perhaps it was simply time for some new blood."

And perhaps that hurt more than Sylvia was letting on. Had being festival director meant so much to her that she'd killed Darcy in anger? I needed to find out.

"I looked at the fairgrounds online in satellite view last night," I said. "I noticed what looked like a bridge from your property to the fairgrounds."

Sylvia brought the motion of her rocking chair to an abrupt halt and backed farther into the seat. Her face tensed.

A tingle ran down my spine. The woman looked guilty, plain and simple. "I bet you could use that bridge to easily access the fairgrounds from your property."

"I...I..." Sylvia glanced down, then back up at us.

My pulse picked up, and I shot a glance at Alice. Was the woman about to admit she'd used the bridge to access the fairgrounds and kill Darcy?

Sylvia's chest caved with an exhale. "I know that bridge probably violates some statute or other. Back when my husband was alive and my son was in high school, the two of them built it for me as a surprise when I was running the festival." Her words tumbled out. "But if a person didn't know where it starts across the river, I don't think they'd ever find it. And it's got a gate with a padlock on the fairgrounds side. At this point, the bridge itself may not even be safe. I haven't used it in years and probably should have someone take it down. Would you ... would you mind not saying anything about it if I promised to call a handyman and have him get right on that today or tomorrow? So it will be down before the festival?"

Alice and I murmured our agreement, but my stomach sank. Sylvia had indeed felt guilty, but that was not the confession I'd hoped to hear.

"Thank you." The lines eased in Sylvia's face. "I know a handyman who's available. I saw him this morning at the drugstore."

I suddenly thought of something. "Sylvia, be sure you check with the police before you remove the bridge."

Her eyebrows scrunched up.

"It might be relevant to the investigation. You don't want removing it to make you look guilty. Someone else could have picked the lock and used it to access the fairgrounds without your knowledge."

"Oh, so the police might want to look for evidence?" Sylvia asked.

"Exactly."

She nodded. "Good idea. But, going back to your earlier question, I'm afraid I didn't see anything helpful on the day of Darcy's murder. I wasn't even here. I went to St. Louis with my retired teachers' group to visit the botanical gardens. Seven of us went up and had the best time."

"That's a pity," I said. In more ways than one. She had an airtight alibi. "I'd hoped you might be able to give us a lead to follow up."

"Sorry," Sylvia said. "All I know is that Bryce Parker is no murderer."

Alice and I thanked her for her time, went back outside, and climbed into Alice's SUV.

"I really had my hopes up there for a moment." I fastened my seatbelt.

"She should get that bridge taken down." Alice started

her car and headed out of the driveway. "But as I suspected, she's not our killer."

"So we've ruled Sylvia out." I crossed my arms over my chest and blew out a frustrated breath. "The festival opens in a little more than forty-eight hours, and we have no idea who the killer is."

## Chapter Eleven

ALICE DROPPED me back at the museum, and as I hurried up the stairs, my phone dinged with a text.

Cleo had sent a photo of Bella with a drooly tennis ball in her mouth, followed by one of Bella curled up on the hardwood floor in front of my fireplace, eyes closed.

*Bella and I squeezed in a game of catch in the backyard. I think I wore her out.*

*Aww.* Cleo was such a dear friend, taking time to play with Bella. I went into my office and dove into preparing for the donor video call. By the time three o'clock rolled around, I had a short PowerPoint presentation ready that showed the impact his gift could make.

An hour later, I had his assurances that he'd be putting a large check in the mail. I hung up, let out a whoop, and shared the good news with Rodney and Imani. I was giving Imani the play-by-play of how I'd made the request when my phone rang. The caller ID read "Dogwood Springs Veterinary Clinic."

I excused myself, answered, and started walking toward my office.

"Libby? This is Madison Thompson. From the vet clinic?"

"Oh, hi."

"Remember how you asked yesterday if Zoe or I had any idea who might have killed Darcy?"

I closed my office door and sat at my desk. "Yes."

"Well, I didn't mean to be eavesdropping, but... Have you ever had a situation where you were sitting there minding your own business and someone started saying something you knew you weren't meant to hear, but you couldn't help it?"

"I have." Just last night at the Pit & Pickle.

"Today after lunch, Aaron Eckhart brought his dog in because his paw got hurt. When Aaron was sitting in the waiting room, I overheard him on the phone."

A niggle of interest ran down my spine. "What did he say?"

"I had to kind of piece it together since I only caught one side of the conversation, but apparently there's a house in town he really wanted to buy, that cute little blue one on Kingley Avenue. It has sentimental value to his girlfriend because her grandmother once owned it. He wanted to buy it and then propose."

"Oh, that's sweet." If the girlfriend wasn't ready to marry him before, that would definitely win her heart.

"It is, except his credit rating is bad. He went to talk to Darcy at the bank where his girlfriend works as a last resort. Somehow, Darcy made him believe it was going to work out, but last Friday she denied his loan. After he'd already told his girlfriend he was getting the house and proposed."

"Ooh. That sounds awkward."

"He was furious. So furious, I guess, that he didn't realize I could hear every word. No one else was in the waiting room, but he'd seen me behind the counter when he came in. He said whoever killed Darcy had done the whole town a favor."

"Whoa. That's pretty harsh," I said. "Like maybe he was the one who killed her."

"That's exactly what I thought," Madison said.

I thanked her for telling me and hung up.

Time to talk to Aaron.

For a moment I sat there, slumped in my chair, tapping a pen on the desk.

I'd rather meet Aaron in a public park during his work shift than later at his home. And my fear that someone else might get killed before the festival began, or during it, was strong enough that I'd be willing to leave work at four and take an hour of vacation time to do so.

The problem was that Dogwood Springs had lots of parks. How could I know which one Aaron was working in today? I tapped the pen again.

Suddenly, I sat upright. Since I'd grown up in Columbus, a good-sized city, I sometimes forgot how interconnected people were in the little town of Dogwood Springs. I texted

Cleo to see if she knew anyone who worked for the parks department.

Sure enough, she did. Within five minutes, I knew that Aaron was working again at the fairgrounds today.

Unfortunately, neither Cleo nor any of my other friends was free to go with me to talk to him. I didn't want to take foolish risks and be alone—even at the fairgrounds—with a possible killer. I was pretty sure, though, that other people would be around, with the festival starting so soon. To be extra careful, I'd make sure my pepper spray was in my purse.

I told Imani and Rodney I was leaving early and drove home.

Bella met me the second I walked in my kitchen door, barking and circling me with her tail swooshing back and forth.

Logically, of course, I knew she couldn't tell time. I'd noticed, though, that even on the weekends, she seemed to sense when it was five fifteen, the time I normally arrived home and fed her. Today she seemed so happy to see me, I wouldn't have been surprised if she knew I was home earlier than normal.

I let her out briefly, then called her back inside.

She looked at the cabinet with the dog food and tipped her head as if asking if dinner would also be early.

"Four fifteen is too early to eat, Bella." I picked up my purse and unhooked her leash from where it hung by the refrigerator. "How about a ride in the car?"

She galloped to the door.

I avoided downtown and soon pulled into the parking lot near the stage at the fairgrounds. I let Bella out of the car and hooked on her leash.

She gazed about, nose twitching one direction, then another. Probably picking up the scent of freshly mown grass and lilacs.

As I'd expected, activity at the fairgrounds had picked up. Tents and food trucks were supposed to be in place by four tomorrow afternoon, but a few vendors had already begun setting up. One brave soul, who must not have expected much wind, had already raised a tent. I heard people talking in the distance, spotted Maria Wilder of Wild Woods Winery over near the wine and beer garden, and, somewhere off in the distance, caught the sound of someone edging and trimming weeds.

Hopefully, that someone was Aaron.

"Let's see if we can find him." I gave a gentle tug on Bella's leash and started toward the closest vendor area.

As we passed the restrooms, a huge, bald man—probably fifty years old, six feet, eight inches tall, and 300 pounds—walked out. His worn jeans hung low beneath his belly, and his T-shirt strained at his girth.

"Well, hey there, little lady, that's a fine-looking dog you've got." He let Bella sniff his hand then tapped his chest. "Jimbo Rollins, purveyor of the finest fried macaroni and cheese in the land."

I introduced myself and Bella and said I was on the festival steering committee. "I remember Harry mentioning you. You're one of the vendors from out of town, aren't you?"

"I am indeed. Good man, Harry. Said I was welcome to come early and park my vehicle on the far side of the lot near the barns for a night or two before the festival."

"Of course." Harry had explained that some out-of-town vendors would camp at the fairgrounds during the event. "It's been nice meeting you. Hope you sell lots of fried macaroni and cheese."

He grinned, displaying a gold tooth.

Bella and I continued on, listening for the sound of yard-care equipment. "We're getting closer, Bella."

Once we passed a big oak, I saw someone bent over, trimming grass near the gravel between the two vendor areas. I couldn't see the person's head, but I spotted jeans, blond hair, and the neon yellow T-shirt of the parks department.

*Aaron.* I walked closer and waved to get his attention over the noise of the trimmer.

He straightened, shut off the machine, and walked toward me.

"I'm Libby Ballard. I'm on the festival steering committee. We met when Darcy was, uh, found."

His expression grew more serious. "Yeah. I remember you." He took off his gloves, then unwrapped a toothpick from his pocket and, holding it by the wrapper, slid it in his mouth.

"This may sound a little weird, but my dog is a patient at Dogwood Springs Veterinary." I tipped my head toward

Bella. "I find it hard to believe that Dr. Parker is a murder suspect. I, uh, I wondered if you happened to see anything unusual that day?"

His eyebrows drew together, and he chewed on the toothpick.

"Maybe something minor that didn't seem worth mentioning to the police." I twisted the end of Bella's leash between my hands. "Darcy interacted with lots of people at the bank with loans and such. Maybe one of them had a reason to kill her."

Aaron's jaw grew tight, and color rose up from the collar of his T-shirt until his whole face was red. He spat the toothpick on the ground. "Doesn't that bank know anything about privacy?" he bellowed.

Beside me, Bella's body tensed.

My throat tightened, and I edged back. I must have been out of my mind, coming here to confront a possible killer. Was anyone close enough that they'd hear me if I called for help?

*No.*

With as little motion as possible, I slid my hand into my purse and began feeling around for my pepper spray. I was such an idiot. I'd been too distracted by meeting Jimbo to have it in my hand first.

"That's what you're hinting at, isn't it?" Aaron's voice grew even louder. "You're accusing me of killing Darcy because she denied my loan. You've got no—"

Bella barked, then growled at him.

Behind me, I heard someone whistling loudly. *Saved!*

"Everything all right, Libby?" Jimbo ambled up beside me.

Aaron looked away, his shoulders sagging. After a second, he turned back to face me. "Sorry." He shook his head rapidly, and his whole demeanor changed, the anger fading quickly. "It's not your fault. I just don't like the fact that the bank seems to have spread my personal financial business all over town."

Should I tell him that it wasn't the bank's fault, that he shouldn't talk so loudly on his cell phone?

*No, probably not.*

"You all good, buddy?" Jimbo gave Aaron a pointed look.

Aaron nodded, and Bella's stance relaxed.

Jimbo hitched up his jeans and walked past us. "Just yell if you need me, Libby."

"You won't need him. I'm not the killer." Aaron scratched the back of his neck. "Darcy denying my loan was no big deal. I got a loan for the house I wanted from another bank."

Well, that shot my latest theory.

"I do agree with you, though," he added. "I don't think Bryce Parker is a murderer, either. I wouldn't think someone who could kill a person would be so gentle with my dog."

"Well, if you didn't kill Darcy, and Bryce didn't kill her, somebody must have," I said. "I just wish I knew who."

"I told the police who I thought did it, but I guess they ignored me."

"Who?" I stepped closer.

"Cameron Sidwell, that guy Darcy worked with at the bank."

Cameron? I'd barely considered him a suspect. "Why? Was there something unusual going on at the bank?"

"There was something going on between him and Darcy." Aaron raised both eyebrows. "But it wasn't at the bank if you know what I mean."

My mind tried to process what he was saying. "You mean he and Darcy..."

"Yep," Aaron said. "She was cheating on Bryce while they were engaged."

*Holy cow.* "How do you know this?"

"Because I run a landscaping business on the side, and I do Cameron's yard every week. When his wife took their daughter out of town to go shopping or do those cheerleading competitions, Cameron used to have Darcy over."

An uneasy feeling pinched at my shoulders. If Darcy was having an affair and Bryce found out, wouldn't that give him a real motive for killing her? "So why would Cameron want to kill her?"

"My girlfriend is a teller at the bank. Apparently, when Darcy and Bryce set a wedding date, she broke things off with Cameron. He got really angry and made a scene at the bank after closing one evening. But enough people were there that Bryce heard about it and learned about the affair."

"That's why he broke up with Darcy for good," I said slowly.

"Yep." Aaron shrugged. "Can't blame him. How could he trust her after she cheated on him when she was his fiancée?"

"The police might see that as more motive for Bryce."

"Maybe," Aaron agreed. "I still can't picture Bryce killing anyone. Cameron, on the other hand, has got quite a temper. He's kind of a jerk. And you saw him here that day, same as me."

"I did." Cameron had looked ill at ease when Detective Harper talked with him, I remembered. He'd said he was worried about his stepdaughter, but maybe he was really nervous because he was Darcy's murderer. "Wow. Well, thanks for talking with me, Aaron. I'll check into Cameron."

He gave me a thumbs-up.

I tugged on Bella's leash, and we headed back toward my car.

# Chapter Twelve

"YOU'VE GOT to be kidding me!" Cleo jammed her hands onto her hips. "Darcy cheated on Bryce before they were even married?"

"That's what Aaron said." I leaned back against her kitchen counter. I'd run up the back stairs with Bella as soon as I got home.

"I bet he didn't tell us because he was embarrassed." Cleo gestured to the chair across from her at her kitchen table.

Or maybe because he knew it made him look guilty, I thought as I sat down. "If he didn't tell us, he probably didn't tell Detective Harper, either. If the detective finds out, it will make him suspect Bryce even more."

"But we know Bryce didn't do it." Cleo stated it like it was an incontrovertible fact, like the existence of gravity.

I did think Cameron was a good suspect, the best lead

we'd had yet. Still, I wondered if we needed to consider the possibility that Bryce might have been the killer.

"Aaron is probably right," Cleo continued. "Cameron is the killer. It makes sense. If Darcy ended their relationship and he was mad about it, he could have been angry enough to kill."

I thought for a moment. "You know, from what Bryce told us, he and Darcy broke up Saturday night. There is a possibility that Cameron heard they broke up on Sunday morning and tried to get back together with her. Maybe he thought, if she were no longer engaged to Bryce, she'd look at their affair differently. But then she rejected him again."

"One rejection on top of another." Cleo nodded. "Even more reason to kill her. But how do we get Detective Harper to seriously consider Cameron as a suspect when he's so fixated on Bryce as the killer?" She ran one finger along her jaw, thinking. "If you and I snuck into Cameron's house and found some evidence—"

I held up a hand to stop her. "How would we get into his house? Breaking and entering might not look good on a museum director's résumé."

"What if he told someone he did it, and we can get them to tell us?"

"If he confessed that he murdered Darcy to someone, I bet they would have already gone to the police. Besides, how would we know who to ask?"

Cleo frowned.

I saw one option, which was risky. But I also suspected Detective Harper would simply roll his eyes at me if I told him our suspicions with no proof. "The only way we can convince Detective Harper for sure is if we somehow trick Cameron into confessing and we get it recorded."

"Perfect!" Cleo exclaimed.

*Aaargh.* My chest grew tight. I should never have mentioned that idea. A trio of warnings echoed in my brain —Sam's, Detective Harper's, Aaron's. And they only got louder when I remembered the wound on the top of Darcy's head.

On the other hand, if we were very, very careful, the plan might work. And the clock was ticking, every second getting closer to the start of the festival on Friday morning. "You'd come with me?" I asked Cleo.

"Try to stop me," she said. "You be in charge of questioning him and recording the conversation on your phone. I'll find out where he lives and then be ready with pepper spray and my best karate kick."

The tightness in my chest eased a bit. Cleo had taken self-defense when she lived in New York. And there'd be two of us, and we'd be catching him unaware. I stood up. "It's a plan. Let's meet a little after seven. That should give us both time to eat dinner and get our courage up. And give me time to think what to say."

A few minutes past seven thirty, Cleo parked her Jeep on the street in front of Cameron's house. It was located in an upscale neighborhood, not far from where Alice lived. From the complicated roofline to the arched windows and over-sized front door to the obsessively trimmed and mulched boxwoods, everything about the place screamed money.

"We'll ask him to walk outside with us before we bring up the murder, right?" I had no desire to be the reason that Cameron's wife or stepdaughter learned about his affair. In front of them, I planned to act as if I was hoping the bank might contribute to the museum.

"You're doing all the talking, remember?" Cleo made a show of zipping her lips.

"Great." I climbed out, and we walked up the flagstone path to the front porch.

Once I reached the door, though, I just stood there, looking at the classy porch furniture and a wooden plaque on the door that said "Welcome, friends." From inside, I heard what sounded like a TV.

Finally, I drew in a deep breath and knocked.

The TV went silent, and the same dark-haired girl I'd seen at the fairgrounds, Noelle, answered almost immediately. She wore an outfit entirely composed of upscale clothing brands. Even I recognized the latest trends and the money that had been thrown at them.

"Oh," she said, sounding disappointed. "I thought you were my study group." The smell of microwave popcorn wafted out. She'd probably been preparing it for her friends.

"Sorry," I said. "This is Cleo Anderson, and I'm Libby Ballard."

The girl's face brightened. "You run the museum with those cool old-time dresses."

"Oh, I'm glad you like them." I had a real thing for historic clothing, too. It was what had interested me in museum work in the first place. "I, uh, I was hoping to talk to your dad. Is he home?"

I peeked behind her, into a two-story entryway with gleaming hardwood.

She shook her head. "He just left. He didn't want to, but he's helping Aunt Eileen park the Pit & Pickle food truck at the fairgrounds. She dropped off a car for him and went back to the restaurant. He's driving out the food truck. She says she can't back that thing into the slot she's assigned."

"Thanks. We'll try to catch him there."

Noelle waved and shut the door.

And Cleo and I walked back to her Jeep.

Ten minutes later, Cleo pulled into the parking lot near the stage at the fairgrounds. We were the only car in the lot.

She glanced over at me. "Ready?"

I held up my phone and switched on the recording app. We'd have a lot of dead air while we walked to the food truck, but at least I wouldn't get nervous and forget to turn it on. "Ready. And I know where the Pit & Pickle truck will be parked. Right next to the spot where the museum will have its tent."

We got out and walked toward the vendor areas.

The sun had slipped below the horizon, and the temperature had cooled considerably from when I'd been here earlier. Humidity from the recent rain still hung in the air, making it even chillier, and I wished I'd brought a light jacket. Frogs peeped softly, probably hanging out along the river, and, although we didn't see anyone, somewhere in the distance, music played. The locals might have gone home for the night, but at least one vendor from out of town was around.

"The Pit & Pickle truck should be on the far side of the smaller vendor area, where there's that wide gravel path you can drive through."

When we came to the far edge of the smaller vendor area, Cleo glanced over at me. "Do you know what you're going to say?"

I nodded and pointed. "Look. The Pit & Pickle truck's already here." It was neatly parked, but I could understand why Eileen had handed off the job of getting it positioned. With all the flags in place to mark where each tent or truck should go, it would have been like parallel parking a fifteen-person van. Way beyond my skill level. "I hope Cameron hasn't already left."

We both walked faster. As we drew closer, I saw that Eileen had made a large sign out of poster board and taped it over the Pit & Pickle logo on the side of the vehicle. Beside the words "Fresh, Hot, Funnel Cakes," she'd drawn what I guessed was supposed to be a funnel cake. Mostly it looked like squiggles.

Artistic or not, she was doing her part to help the festival raise money for the Good Neighbor Fund.

We reached the side of the truck with the service

window, and Cleo pointed. "The door on the back is open," she whispered. "Cameron must still be here."

"Hello?" I called. "Cameron? We were hoping to talk with you for a moment."

No answer.

Cleo and I walked around to the back of the truck, and I peered inside. The last light from the sun was fading, and the interior was completely hidden by shadows. "I don't think he's here, Cleo. Maybe he forgot to lock the door, and it fell open?" I wasn't sure what equipment Eileen had in her truck for making funnel cakes, but I imagined there might be big fryers that she wouldn't want stolen. "Let's see if we can figure out a way to lock it."

"Good idea." Cleo pulled out her phone. "Let me give you some light." She turned on the flashlight app and pointed the beam inside the truck.

I'd been right. The beam glinted off a huge, gleaming fryer.

"Hold on," Cleo said. "I'll angle it so you can see the door lock." She moved the light, and the beam passed across the floor of the truck.

Where Cameron lay motionless.

A large gash cut deep into his head, and his hands, white dress shirt, and the floor of the food truck were covered with blood.

## Chapter Thirteen

I SCREAMED, jerked back, and grabbed Cleo's arm to pull her away from the truck.

Once we were a few feet away, my heart thudded in my chest, and I gasped for breath.

"Is he dead?" she asked, with a tremor in her voice.

"I think so." No person could lose that much blood and still be alive.

Cleo and I exchanged uneasy glances.

Two seconds ticked by, then three. A cold breeze cut right through my clothes, and out on Hartley Road, a semi loudly braked as it headed down a hill.

I looked toward the back of the food truck and let out a shaky breath. "I'll see if there's a pulse. The festival committee has security patrols tonight, but they don't start until ten. You'd better call the police."

Cleo nodded.

By now, night had completely fallen, and the moon was

mostly behind a cloud. I knew, from what we'd been told on the steering committee, that the fairgrounds had a vast lighting system. Unfortunately, the vendor areas all ran on one big switch, which was currently off.

I dug my own phone from my purse to use as a flashlight, stopped the recording app, and set my purse in the grass near the rear tire of the truck.

Cleo was already talking to the 911 operator. "We're checking," she said into her phone.

I turned on the flashlight app and hurried up the narrow metal steps to the back of the truck. The metallic smell of blood mixed with the faint aroma of barbecue, a combination that made me slightly nauseated. Or maybe it was the sight of all that blood. My hands trembled, and my flashlight beam jiggled across Cameron's body. Carefully, so I wouldn't step in blood, I crept closer and gingerly felt for a pulse at his neck.

Even after I tried three times, I couldn't find a pulse.

I hurried out of the truck. Just as I hit the ground and shook my head at Cleo, letting her know Cameron was dead, I heard footsteps running toward us.

Cleo, still on the phone with 911, looked at me with wide eyes, and drew herself up taller, muscles taut.

My heart sped, and I dug in my purse for my pepper spray.

"Is everybody okay?" Jimbo asked as he appeared from the larger vendor area, carrying a flashlight. "I heard a scream."

I exhaled, but Cleo remained on alert. Jimbo seemed

even bulkier than he had when I'd met him, and he did look a little frightening.

"That was me you heard scream," I told him. "Cleo, this is Jimbo. Jimbo, Cleo." I glanced over at the food truck. "There's a man dead. In there."

Jimbo gave a tight nod.

Cleo held the phone away from her mouth. "The police are on their way. Two minutes out."

I shook my head, trying to purge the memory of all that blood. It didn't work. My heart was racing, and I still felt sick to my stomach. Another death, just as we'd feared.

Poor Cameron was not a murderer at all, just a man who'd been concerned about his stepdaughter, a man who'd tried to help his aunt. A man who'd ended up dead.

More than anything, I wanted to run home, take a hot shower, and hide under the covers. What were Cleo and I doing here? Why had I put myself in a position to find my second dead body at the fairgrounds in four days?

If I'd had any sense, I'd have stayed home with Bella.

The wail of sirens rang out, faintly at first, then louder.

I glanced toward the road, and when I looked back, Jimbo was gone. Despite his size, he'd melted into the night without me even knowing.

"Who was that Jimbo guy?" Cleo whispered.

I explained, but she didn't look reassured. And my mind

raced. Why had he left? Had I been wrong to trust him? Had he been the person who killed Cameron?

On the other end of Cleo's phone call, I heard the murmur of a voice.

"Tell them we're between the vendor areas, at the Pit & Pickle truck," Cleo told the operator.

Somewhere nearby, an owl cried out, and a shiver ran down my spine.

Seconds later, a police car drove up the gravel path between the two vendor areas. Two car doors slammed shut, and the beam of a powerful flashlight bounced off the grass. "Are you two all right?" a man in a police uniform called out.

"Yes," I replied. "We're the ones who called you."

The cop ran closer and raised the flashlight enough that I could see his face. I recognized him as Officer Tate.

Officer Davis, a younger officer I'd also met before, joined him. The paramedics soon followed and climbed into the food truck.

As I'd suspected, Cameron was dead. The paramedics gave no indication they might try to save him.

He was really gone.

Poor Noelle. And her poor mom.

"I'll need to get some information from you both," Officer Tate said.

My knees suddenly felt wobbly. "Rodney already brought over some metal folding chairs from the museum." I pointed to the stack piled under a tarp in the next vendor spot. "Could we sit down?"

"Of course." He took my arm and set up a chair for me and one for Cleo. Once we were seated, he insisted that I place my head between my knees for a few minutes. It might have been excessive, but I didn't protest. Normally, I was okay with the sight of blood, but I guess everybody had a limit.

He even called the paramedics over to check me, but after a few minutes, I felt steadier.

Suddenly, the lights in both vendor areas came on.

A second later, Detective Harper strode toward us, dress shirt sleeves rolled up, eyebrows bristling. I had a strong suspicion he was not happy to see me at another crime scene.

"Libby ... Cleo." He nodded and looked us over. "You're both unharmed?"

We assured him we were all right.

His mouth twisted to one side, and he pulled out a small, black notebook and pen. "Tell me what happened."

In bits and pieces, with each of us interrupting the other, Cleo and I explained what we had found. We told him everything—the way the door had been open, that we'd thought we should lock the truck up for Eileen, and how we'd found her nephew dead. I added that I had checked for a pulse, and Cleo had called for help. We also told him about Jimbo, and how he'd suddenly disappeared.

Detective Harper's eyes narrowed. "The fried mac and cheese guy?"

I nodded.

"I talked to him earlier," Detective Harper said. "I doubt

he'd have a reason to kill Cameron or Darcy, being an out-of-towner, but running off doesn't make him look especially trustworthy."

I kept silent, but I agreed with him.

"So now we come to another big question." The detective crossed his arms over his chest. "What exactly were you ladies doing here?"

I shot a look at Cleo. I couldn't lie to the police. "We, um, we came to talk to Cameron. His stepdaughter told us he was here, parking the Pit & Pickle truck for his aunt."

The detective made a note. "Eileen Davidson owns this vehicle?"

"She does," I said. "She told Harry she'd sell funnel cakes instead of barbecue because the festival already had a barbecue vendor."

He scribbled something else in his notebook. "And you came out here at night to talk to Cameron because...?" The detective looked at me, then Cleo, then me again.

"Because we know Bryce wasn't the person who killed Darcy." Cleo's words burst out, loud and defensive. "I guess nobody's told you, but she and Cameron were having an affair. She broke things off with him, and he made a real scene at the bank."

"So you decided Cameron was the killer?" The detective's voice rose, his tone even more incredulous. "And you thought it was a good idea to come talk to him alone, here in the dark, at the practically deserted fairgrounds?"

"It wasn't dark when we got here," I mumbled.

"Frankly, I don't care." The detective blew out a heavy

breath, the way I'd imagine a bull might breathe right before it charged at someone and gored them. "I'll have you know that my team and I were aware of the relationship between Cameron and Darcy, and why Bryce ended his engagement to her."

"So you agree Cameron seemed like a viable suspect?" I said.

"As I've told you in the past, Miss Ballard, you are not a member of law enforcement. You should not be making a list of suspects or trying to solve a murder case." He glared at me. "You do realize that whoever bashed Cameron in the head could have easily done the same to you?"

I shifted my weight, and the folding chair squeaked. "Yeah." I thought about telling him that we'd had pepper spray and that I'd had the voice recorder app running on my phone. But I knew it wouldn't make a difference.

"If you suspected Cameron," Cleo said, "why did you let the whole town think Bryce was the killer?"

The detective's lips tightened. "Cameron wasn't my primary suspect. The man had his stepdaughter with him here at the fairgrounds the day Darcy was killed. In my experience, I've never known someone to commit murder with their own child around."

*Hmmm.* There was some logic in that.

"As a law enforcement professional"—he gave me a long look—"I've been working methodically, checking each alibi. For instance, last night I verified that Harry was on the phone with Jimbo when Darcy was killed."

I nodded. In my view, though, an alibi from Jimbo now

seemed less solid, given how he'd run off when he heard sirens.

"And if I needed any further proof that Bryce was our number one suspect," Detective Harper said, "I got it tonight. He was one of only a handful of people at the fairgrounds at the time of the first murder. And his fiancée and the man she was having an affair with are both dead, both killed in the same way. How many people in this town had a reason to hate the two of them as much as he did?"

Cleo opened her mouth, then closed it.

I shot her a rueful look. Oh, we still had other suspects. It wasn't an absolute given that Bryce was the killer. But as much as Cleo might hate to admit it, Detective Harper was right.

Bryce had an excellent motive for killing Darcy.

And Cameron.

## Chapter Fourteen

AS SOON AS Cleo and I got home, I let Bella out, then contacted the rest of my friends to let them know we'd found Cameron dead.

Both Sam and Alice were immediately concerned that Cleo and I had taken too great a risk. In retrospect, it was clear that our plan had not been a good one, and I gladly agreed when Alice asked me to promise not to interview suspects in deserted locations.

Then I arranged to meet everyone—except Zeke, who, of course, had to be at school on a Thursday—at the Dogwood Café for lunch the next day to discuss the investigation. I hated to leave Zeke out, but with all festival tents required to be set up by four tomorrow afternoon and the gates opening to the public at nine Friday morning, we needed to act quickly.

I drove to work on Thursday to allow me to run home quickly to check on Bella. The whole way in, I thought about Cameron. I hadn't known him, but his death would make a big hole in the lives of his family and friends. Across town, I knew people were shocked and grieving, trying to wrap their brains around the loss. And somewhere, the killer probably sat smugly, believing he or she would never be caught.

For the morning, I had to focus on the museum's preparations for the festival, but at lunch, my friends and I would do our best to figure out who that culprit was.

Imani and I spent the morning loading her minivan with items for the museum's display at the festival. Finally, a few minutes before noon, we slid the last box into place. I wiped my brow, and Imani fanned her face with one hand. If you were simply standing around, the weather was perfect. If you were working, it was hot. Luckily, it was supposed to cool down a bit before tomorrow.

I zipped over to Elm Street, let Bella out for a moment, then returned my car to the museum and walked to the café.

The outdoor seating area was more crowded than normal, but Alice was already there, sitting at our favorite table. Sam arrived shortly after me, and Cleo rushed up a minute later. We settled in, were served our drinks, and quickly placed our lunch orders. Sam opened the umbrella over our table, providing welcome shade.

The delight I normally felt in eating with my friends at the restaurant I thought of as "our place" was missing. Instead, my shoulders were tense, and I kept finding myself digging my nails into my palms.

Across the table from me, Cleo looked just as ill at ease. As soon as the server left our table, Cleo leaned in. "Bryce has been arrested for Cameron's murder. I don't even know if he'll be let out on bail."

The rest of us sat silent. I was reluctant to tell Cleo, but personally, I felt relieved that Bryce was in custody. If the police thought he'd committed not just one, but two murders, I didn't want him out on the streets.

"I got a call from Harry at work this morning," I said. "The festival is going ahead. Detective Harper seems certain that with Bryce in custody, the people attending the event will be safe."

Alice wrapped her arms across her chest and ran one hand up and down the upper sleeve of her navy and white striped shirt. "We do have to consider the possibility, Cleo, that Detective Harper might be right," she said gently.

Cleo stiffened, and her mouth pinched in.

"I know that's not what you want to hear, Cleo," Sam said. "But I agree with Alice. Bryce has a strong motive for killing both Darcy and Cameron, and, although we don't know about the second murder, we know he was at the fairgrounds when Darcy was killed."

Interesting. Everyone but Cleo was thinking the same way I was. "We also know that Detective Harper has been investigating other possibilities. He told us last night he'd looked into Cameron, and he verified that Harry was on the phone with a vendor when Darcy was killed."

Cleo started to speak but stopped. Our server was back in record time with our meals.

He must have sensed the strain at the table because he served Alice's chef salad, Cleo and Sam's burgers and fries, and my club sandwich and slaw without a word, except to ask if we wanted anything else. We told him we were fine, and he hurried away.

"Okay," Cleo said. "I know you all think I'm not seeing things clearly because I'm still in love with Bryce—which, by the way, I'm not—but that's not it. I know him. I've known him longer than I've known any of you. How can I explain it?" She tapped her nails on the table and looked at Sam and me. "Would you believe me if I told you Alice committed a murder?"

"Never," I said.

Sam, who had just taken a big bite of his burger, shook his head.

Cleo made a gun with her thumb and forefinger, pretended to shoot it, and blew off the imaginary barrel. "Even if she was found, standing over a dead body with a gun in her hand?"

I looked over at Sam, then at Alice. "No. Never."

"Thanks," Alice said softly.

"Now you understand how I feel about Bryce." Cleo squirted a large blob of ketchup onto her plate and set the bottle down with a *thump*. "He's not the killer."

I took the frilly toothpick out of one section of my club sandwich and rolled it between my fingers. Had I been taking the easy way out, suspecting Bryce? Possibly. I certainly hadn't been trusting Cleo's judgment, which I should have.

And she made a good point. If she'd dated Bryce and known him for years, she would know him even better than she knew me, and she was my best friend.

"Okay." I looked over at her. "We're taking him off the suspect list entirely." I pushed the tomato slice that was trying to escape back into my club sandwich, took a bite, and thought as I chewed. The more I thought, the tighter my shoulders grew. "That means we're back to square one. We've talked with each of our other suspects and ruled them out. So we have no idea who the killer is."

"And no idea if people will be safe at the Dogwood Festival," Alice added.

"Which starts tomorrow morning," I said.

Fear flickered in Cleo's eyes.

Sam squared his shoulders.

And Alice's eyebrows pinched together.

"All right, then." I sat up taller. "Let's review our possible suspects one by one and consider what motive they each might have had for killing Cameron."

"We started out with seven suspects," Sam said. "Bryce, Harry, Aaron, Sylvia, Cameron, Zoe, and Madison."

"Cameron's dead." I wiped some mayonnaise off my fingers with my napkin. "If we rule out Bryce—"

"And Sylvia because she was in St. Louis," Cleo added.

"That brings us down to four," Sam said.

Alice sat down her fork in her chef salad. "Do we know when Cameron was killed?"

"Pretty much," Cleo said. "We know he left home about seven thirty, and Libby and I found his body about eight."

"Then we can eliminate Harry," Alice said. "I was picking up a carry-out order for a late dinner, and I saw him sitting in his car at the back of the Pit & Pickle lot right in the middle of that timeframe. He wouldn't have had time to get to the fairgrounds and kill Cameron."

"Are you sure it was him that you saw?" Sam asked.

"Yes. He was looking away from me, toward the trees at the back of the lot, but it was definitely his car, and I heard him on the phone, verifying details with out-of-town vendors. I recognized his voice."

Drat. I'd thought, since Jimbo might not be the most trustworthy person and he gave Harry an alibi for Darcy's murder, that maybe we could reconsider Harry as a suspect. Alice, on the other hand, was an incredibly trustworthy person. If she said Harry was at the Pit & Pickle at the time Cameron was killed, Harry was in the clear.

"That only leaves three suspects." Sam counted them off on his fingers. "Zoe, Madison, and Aaron."

I took a sip of my iced tea. None of those three seemed like a killer to me. Aaron had gotten angry with me, but I, too, would have been upset if I'd thought my personal financial information was being spread around town. And Zoe and Madison seemed like genuinely nice people. But one of the three must have killed not only Darcy but also Cameron.

"As for a motive for killing Cameron," I finally said. "They each could have had the same one. If Cameron saw one of them kill Darcy or saw something that later let him figure out who the killer was, the murderer might have killed him to silence him."

"That's logical." Sam nodded and took a bite of his burger.

"But how are we going to prove that?" Cleo sighed. "We can't ask Cameron what he saw. He's dead."

That did complicate things. "I think we need to go back to what they told us when we talked with them after Darcy's murder," I said. "One of them had to be lying. We just have to learn which one."

Everyone else murmured their agreement.

"Well..." Cleo took a quick sip of her diet Dr. Pepper. "Both Madison and Zoe rely a lot on that queen candidate, Kayla, for their alibi." Cleo hesitated. "I know Zeke believes Zoe is innocent, but I think we should ask him to talk to Kayla to verify their story."

"That's a good idea," Alice said. "Kayla might talk better one-on-one with him."

"What about Aaron?" Sam dragged a French fry through ketchup and munched on it, eyes narrowed.

"He told me the fact that Darcy denied his loan wasn't that big a deal because he got a loan from somewhere else," I said.

"If he did, that little blue house he wanted should be under contract or at least be in the process—that 'contract pending' stage." Alice glanced around to see if we knew what she meant.

We all nodded.

"I've got a friend who's a real estate agent," Alice continued. "I should be able to find out if Aaron's buying that house."

"That would be great," I said. "If we find out that someone was lying, we'll know who to look into more closely."

"You know..." Alice stabbed a chunk of boiled egg from her salad with her fork. "If Cameron's wife, Tiffany knew about the affair, she would also be a strong suspect. And I've heard rumors that their marriage was pretty rocky. One person even said she and Noelle might be better off without Cameron in their lives."

"Maybe she killed him, but I don't see how she could have killed Darcy," I said. "No one saw her car at the fairgrounds when Darcy was killed."

"Could she have slipped in and out of the parking lot quickly and not been seen?"

"She drives an enormous, bright-red SUV," Cleo said. "Her car would have been noticed if she were there. And even if Hartley Road were safe for walking or biking, I can't see Tiffany doing either of those things. She's more of a valet-service kind of gal."

"And both murders were committed in the same way." Alice's forehead creased. "So that does make it seem like the same person committed both crimes."

"I agree," Cleo said. "I sure like that idea a lot better than the option of two murderers on the loose in Dogwood Springs."

"Me too," I said. "Although we can't completely rule out

Tiffany in Cameron's murder. Maybe she did manage to slip in and out of the park unseen. But how can we find out?"

Alice, Sam, and Cleo exchanged glances.

"I don't know her or her friends very well," Cleo said.

Alice shook her head. "Me either. But I can see if any of my friends are friends with her friends. Maybe someone would know something."

That didn't sound like a very solid way to get information, but I didn't have a better idea. "It's at least a place to start." I picked up the last quarter of my club sandwich and took a bite. "This has to be the most confusing case we've ever tried to solve."

The others murmured in agreement.

We had almost nothing to go on, and we had only—

I stopped and counted it up in my head.

Twenty hours before the festival began.

Chapter Fifteen

BY ONE O'CLOCK I was back at the museum.

Attendance in the morning had been a little higher than average, but nothing unusual. And my friends and I hadn't had much trouble getting a table for lunch at the café.

But according to Rodney and Imani, by three o'clock, Dogwood Springs would be bursting with tourists, all eager for the start of the festival tomorrow.

Imani and I left Rodney and a trio of volunteers in charge of the museum and each drove toward the fairgrounds.

I parked in the main lot. Imani pulled up next to me and I joined her in her minivan. Then, since vendors and exhibitors were allowed to drive to their sites during set up, she navigated her way as close as possible to the museum's tent.

I'd somehow missed the fair last summer, so each time I'd walked around the grounds, they'd been mostly empty.

Not so today.

In addition to vehicles unloading, dozens of people filled the pathways and tents, each busily preparing for tomorrow. The sound of hammering rang through the air as final tents were raised and bunting was hung. Food trucks were already in place. And the scent of hot dogs and hamburgers, which were being sold at cost for the afternoon and evening to volunteers, vendors, and exhibitors, wafted through the air.

As people walked by, I overheard more than one conversation about Bryce, Darcy, and Cameron, but from the snippets I caught, it seemed as if most people, though shocked, had accepted that Bryce was the killer and were trying to move past it.

Despite the recent tragedies, there was a feeling of excitement in the air, as if the town was determined, no matter what, to pull together, to make sure every visitor had a marvelous time, and to ensure that the Good Neighbor Fund was filled to overflowing by the end of the weekend.

Two of my museum board members, Maria Wilder, who owned the local winery, and Andy Lane, a local car dealer, were also on the steering committee with me. They each stopped at the museum's tent to ask if we'd heard that turnout this year was expected to be the highest ever.

A zing of pride shot through me, thinking about what special people we had on our board. Of our six board members, two of them were also taking a big role in this important fundraiser.

For a moment I wondered why Alice didn't take a larger role in the festival. I knew she'd recently registered for two college classes for the fall and one for the summer, but she was the backbone of many volunteer organizations in town. Then I realized the difference. The festival was a once-a-year volunteer event for most people. Alice was a key volunteer in groups that needed help every week of the year. Knowing her kind heart, she probably intentionally left the festival as a place for others to shine.

Once Imani and I had unloaded her van, she drove it back to the main parking lot, and we began setting up.

Our tent consisted of a white canopy top with the same fabric draped down the back of the tent and the back half of each side. The front of the tent and the front half of the sides were open.

First, we set up the four big tables we'd been given and arranged them in a wide U, with the opening toward the back. We left enough space on each side so that we could slip in between the partial side of the tent and the edge of the table. Then, on the tables, we set up our displays, including one about the history behind the dogwoods in town and the Dogwood Festival, and a triple-chance guess-the-antiques exhibit.

I couldn't have been prouder as I set up the information about the dogwoods. The area came by many of its beautiful dogwoods naturally. The large cluster of them near the actual springs outside town, the original Dogwood Springs, had been here years before the town was settled. But it was my own great-great-grandmother, Elsie Dorsett, who had come up with the idea to rebrand—back before rebranding was a word—the little town of Silersville into Dogwood Springs. And it was Great-Great-Grandma Elsie who had ensured that every home in town had a small dogwood and a small hard maple to plant. Those trees, and that vision, were what had helped make Dogwood Springs the charming tourist destination it was today.

The guess-the-antiques exhibit was another favorite of mine. Earlier in the year, after a bit of fun when Rodney tried to come up with an antique Imani and I couldn't identify, we shared the game with museum visitors. It had been a huge hit, and we'd expanded it for the festival. Each of us had picked an antique that we thought might stump visitors.

Rodney had brought in a carved wooden item, about four inches tall and four inches in diameter that was shaped almost like a bell. It had two pieces. The first was the wooden body of the "bell." The second piece was a wooden handle that went through a hole in the top of the bell-shaped base. On the end of the handle was a round disk that met the sides of the bell and had a carving of a cow on the underside.

Imani contributed a pair of vintage gloves, but they were an odd half-glove, half-mitten combination, with each thumb and forefinger separated and the middle finger, ring finger, and pinky all together like in a mitten. They had lace trim at the cuffs and were made of sheer aqua fabric, useless for keeping fingers warm.

And I had dug a porcelain item out of a box in the attic of the museum. It was a two-piece item from 1886, about nine inches high and nine inches in diameter, with a handle on the top of the lid and a handle on one side of the bowl. Both the lid and bowl had pink dahlias painted on them, and the piece had a clear maker's mark.

If someone guessed all three correctly, they would win a year's free admission to the museum. From those winners, we'd draw one name for a grand prize of $100.

Of course, we also had brochures about the museum, along with forms for anyone who wanted to buy a membership, donate, or volunteer.

About three, Eileen Davidson walked up to our display. Her grayish-blond hair hung limp, the lines on her face were more pronounced than they had been when I'd last seen her at the Pit & Pickle, and she had dark circles under her eyes.

Imani and I both expressed our condolences, and Eileen thanked us.

"How are you doing?" I gestured to her food truck, where her nephew had been killed. "This has to be so difficult."

"I think I'm still in shock," she said. "I don't want to pull out of the festival, but I'm not going to be here or at the restaurant for a few days. At least I had everything purchased and stored back at the restaurant before Cameron was killed. And my staff..." She shook her head. "Two of the prep cooks came over and cleaned this place as soon as the police released it. They even loaded in all the non-perishables."

I sank back on my heels. Wow. I would never have dreamed Eileen or her staff would still offer funnel cakes at the festival after Cameron's death. "Is there anything I can do to help?"

"Actually, there is, Libby. That's why I'm here. I've got some of my staff coming out during the festival, but, what with me taking time off and needing my staff to run the restaurant as well as work the festival, I don't have anyone I can ask to sit here and wait to get the truck approved." She glanced over at it. "Andy Lane suggested perhaps I could leave a key with you, you could let the steering committee member in to do the final check, and then you could give it to one of my staff members when they're here tomorrow." She held a key in her hand as if hesitant to offer it to me.

I reached out and took it. "I'd be happy to do that."

"Thank you so much. Maria Wilder is checking the food trucks, and she knows I won't be here. She just has to see that all the ingredients, paper plates and napkins, and signage are in place. Oh, and fire extinguishers."

"Consider it done." I slid the key in my back pocket. "Do I need to let in whoever's working at your truck first thing in the morning?"

"No. We've got more than one key. Just make sure you give that one to one of my staff sometime tomorrow."

"Will do."

She glanced at her watch. "I've got to go. I'm meeting my brother, Cameron's dad, at the funeral home."

Imani and I quietly bid her goodbye and told her we'd be thinking of her and her family. Then, more subdued, we finished preparing our exhibit.

By three thirty, our displays were set up, and—except for one corner of the canopy, which sagged because of a slightly bent tent pole—our exhibit looked good.

Unfortunately, the museum was using one of the loaner tents that belonged to the festival committee. We'd been told upfront that they weren't in the best condition. Unlike a commercial vendor who might use a canopy dozens of times a year, I hadn't been able to justify buying a brand-new canopy for the few times a year the museum might use one.

Eventually, Imani and I agreed that she would try to deal with the sagging corner of the tent, and I would run home to get Bella. Bella and I could wait until the steering committee member in charge of exhibits came by and said we were good to go. Imani could head home early since she, Rodney, and I would be putting in plenty of hours over the weekend at the festival. After our tent was approved, Bella and I could wander the grounds, getting a feel for where everything was, before we went over to Sam's, where we'd been invited for dinner. While I was home, I'd pack water for Bella, her dinner, and a jacket in case temperatures cooled after sunset.

Before I left, I stood for a moment, admiring the museum's displays. All in all, except for the sagging corner, things were going fairly well.

But one space over, the Pit & Pickle food truck sat silent.

The metal flap over the service window was securely latched down. The door was shut tight. And the image of Cameron's body, sprawled dead on the floor of the truck, was seared into my memory.

## Chapter Sixteen

"WE NEED to get over to the museum tent and relieve Imani." I tugged on Bella's leash for the third time.

Despite the increased traffic in town, we'd made it quickly back to the fairgrounds, thanks to a shortcut I knew. Getting from the parking lot to the museum's tent, though, was taking longer than I'd expected.

A woman named JoBeth, who I knew as a local bar owner, had called me over to the tent where she was selling homemade dog treats and offered Bella a sample.

Bella gobbled it down, licked her lips, and raised her head to sniff around the base of the treat canister.

I bought one for Bella to have later. "Your treats are a hit," I told JoBeth.

Bella sat on her haunches, right in front of the canister.

"Thanks." JoBeth tucked a wisp of blond hair that had escaped her ponytail behind her ear. "I've been making strides to improve the bar I got in my divorce, but I don't want to be running it five years from now. It's good money, but my heart's not in it."

"What do you want to do?"

She gestured to the cannister. "Scale up production of these and sell them nationally. I've already found a commercial kitchen I can rent one night a week, starting next month."

"That's wonderful." Good for her, following her dreams. "I expect we might be back to buy more." I grinned and nudged Bella with my foot as I pulled on her collar. "But right now we should go."

Slowly, Bella rose to her feet. She gave one last, longing look at the dog treat stand and walked with me to the museum's tent.

I stepped under the shade of the tent and emptied the water I'd brought in a reusable steel bottle into a bowl for Bella.

"Look at it." Imani pointed toward the sagging corner of the canopy and planted her hands on her hips. "I tried staking a line behind the tent, and it looked right for about two minutes. The ground over there is still wet from the rain on Tuesday, and you can't put the tent stake in very deep because you hit solid rock. I tried moving it to four different places."

"Southern Missouri does have a lot of rocks," I said. Unlike where I'd grown up in Ohio, the topsoil here was thin or, in some places, nonexistent. I studied the situation. "Maybe I could get some longer rope and try to fix it tomorrow morning. You never know, there might be more topsoil farther out."

Imani agreed with the plan and headed home.

Bella and I sat under the canopy, watching people go past our tent. Maria Wilder came by, checked the food truck next door, and gave it the green light. After about ten minutes, the steering committee member in charge of exhibits stopped by and, after frowning at the sagging corner, declared our tent ready for the festival.

I shifted all the display items to the center of the tent and covered them with a huge tarp. I had just finished when my phone dinged with a text from Alice.

*My real estate agent friend works in the same office as the listing agent for the house Aaron wanted to buy. She says someone else is buying it. Based on some paperwork she happened to see, she says Aaron probably didn't get a loan.*

"We're all done here, Bella." I grabbed my big purse. Aaron was most likely somewhere at the fairgrounds, tending to a last-minute crisis. But he might head home at five, and it was already twenty 'til. "We've got some sleuthing to do."

We started near the stage on the west side of the fairgrounds and worked our way in swaths, going from the southern edge of the grounds by Hartley Road to the northern edge by the river, looking for Aaron. Along the way, each time I saw someone I knew, I asked if they had seen him.

No such luck.

The more I thought about it, the more Aaron seemed like the perfect suspect. First of all, he'd lied to me. He hadn't gotten a loan from another bank. So when Darcy denied his loan, it really had been, as Madison said, his last chance. Second, Cameron worked at the same bank as Darcy. I don't know why I hadn't realized it before, but if Aaron killed Darcy because she denied his loan, he might have killed Cameron for a similar reason. Maybe Aaron thought they made the decision together.

But where was he? Was he working at a different park today?

I peered down the walking path that passed in front of the Pit & Pickle truck and the museum tent and—

Wait, there he was. That neon yellow T-shirt was hard to miss.

And what was he doing? Returning to the scene of the crime, the food truck where he'd murdered Cameron last night?

"Bella, let's go." I walked as quickly as I could, dodging people right and left. "Aaron," I cried out. "I need to speak with you."

He looked up with a blatantly guilty expression on his face.

Aha! There was no way he'd try to hurt me with all these crowds of people around. And if I had a chance to question him, I wasn't wasting any time.

I strode up to him and planted my feet. "You said it was

no big deal that Darcy denied your loan, that you'd gotten the money from another bank. But that isn't true."

His forehead bunched up, and he blinked at me, chewing on a toothpick. "Remind me to move my bank and all my financial dealings out of town," he said with a sigh. "Privacy in this town is a joke."

"But why did you lie to me?" I said quickly.

Bella sat to one side, peering at him, as if she, too, wanted an answer.

He reached up, removed the toothpick from his mouth, and tossed it on the ground. "I lied because if you knew the truth, you'd think I killed Darcy. And probably think I killed Cameron as well. Which. I. Didn't." He landed hard on every word. "Neither one of them is to blame for my horrible credit rating."

"But you were here at the park at the time Darcy was murdered."

"I work here." He rolled his eyes. "And a lot of other people were here then too, like you." He gave me a pointed stare. "Maybe you did it."

"I-I—"

"Chill." He blew out an exasperated breath. "I don't believe you're a murderer. But neither am I. If you need proof, I can find three guys I was bowling with when Cameron was killed."

"Oh." That was an easy alibi to check since he'd been in a public place. If he was making up a lie, he'd have chosen something harder to verify. Which meant he wasn't the killer. But there was one thing I didn't understand. "Then why did you look so guilty when I walked up?"

"Because I felt bad that the history museum got the tent canopy with the dented pole. Some woman ran into it last year when she was backing her van up to load up all the stuff she didn't sell. They should have ordered a new one, or at least gotten a replacement part for the pole. That corner was drooping something awful." He pointed. "I fixed it, though."

Sure enough, the corner of the tent was nice and taut. He'd run a narrow rope from the back corner of the canopy to a food truck that sold giant pretzels and was back-to-back with the museum's tent.

"I've got some red triangular flags I'll attach to that rope," he said. "Only vendors and exhibitors are supposed to walk back there, but I don't want anyone to accidentally run into it."

My shoulders drooped. Here he'd been doing a good thing, and I accused him of murder. "I'm so sorry for accusing you. The canopy looks great now. Thank you."

"No worries," he said.

Bella walked over beside him, and he petted her without looking down as if the gesture was automatic, but his mind was elsewhere. After a moment, he spoke. "I still don't believe Bryce is the killer." He shifted his weight and glanced off to one side.

He wanted to say something. I could feel it. I stepped closer. "What are you thinking?"

"I hate to say it," he said in a low voice. "But after I

talked with the guys at the bowling alley, I've been wondering if it might have been Madison Thompson."

"Madison? You mean because of the way Darcy eliminated her daughter from the queen contest?"

"No, because, according to one of the guys I bowl with, Madison has hated Darcy since high school."

I stared at him. "Really?"

He nodded slowly. "My friend said that of all the people in town, no one hated Darcy as much as Madison." He shrugged, walked over to the rope he'd put up, gave it a quick pull, as if making sure it was secure, and walked off.

Wow. So all that business Madison told me about being good friends with Darcy had been a lie.

I paced back and forth in front of the museum's tent, my mind racing. Was there anyone who I'd spoken with who had told me the whole truth?

Apparently not.

But if there was one thing I'd learned since moving to Dogwood Springs, it was that between Alice and Cleo, I had access to information about almost every person in town. I sent a quick text to both of them, asking them to contact anyone they knew who was Darcy's age to learn what had gone on in high school and to see if Madison still hated Darcy.

Within a minute, I got back a thumbs-up emoji from each of them.

I slid my phone in my purse. Thankfully, I could count on my friends to gather information.

Which meant that, for the moment, I'd done all I could.

I checked the museum's tent one last time and gazed over at the Pit & Pickle food truck.

Was Madison the person who had murdered Cameron there last night? Had Cameron seen her kill Darcy? Was something that went on when she and Darcy were in high school a reason to commit murder all these years later?

And, if all of that speculation was wrong, and Madison wasn't the culprit, did that mean Zoe was the killer?

Chapter Seventeen

SAM'S HOUSE, Ashlington, was located west of town off Red Barn Road.

It was a pale peach, two-and-a-half-story Victorian that sat on a ridge and had a big front yard and a long, curving driveway. Its wide front porch arced out to form a rounded entryway with a matching balcony above, and the roofline featured twin chimneys and a turret. A few years ago, when my Aunt Gloria decided to move south, she sold the place to Sam. Since then, he'd done some very tasteful updating, including removing the vivid pink tile in the bathrooms and redoing the entire kitchen.

Ordinarily, between fond memories of visiting Ashlington to see my grandparents when I was a child and the fun times I'd spent there with Sam, simply turning into the long driveway filled my chest with bubbles of happiness. Today, I just felt tense. Aaron had lied to me. Madison may have lied to me. Who knew who else may have covered their tracks, either to keep unrelated secrets hidden or because they were the killer?

Bella, though, was unphased by all the deception.

As soon as I opened the car door, she hopped out into Sam's driveway, did two laps around his large front yard, and raced to the door, barking.

I knocked, but he didn't answer. When he'd texted to invite me, he'd said that he might be caught up in something and that if he didn't come to the door, I should come on in.

I calmed Bella down and stepped inside. I was about to call out a hello when I heard Sam talking with someone in his office.

"Sounds good," he said. I heard a chair creak and then he stepped into the hall.

I looked back toward his office to see who he'd been with.

"It's just me. I was on a video call," he said. "Hey, I had intended to cook, but I got swamped at the university. The end of the semester is insane. Anyway, I picked up dinner from our favorite Mexican place."

"Thank you. That sounds wonderful." Even if we hadn't yet managed to find the killer, I was incredibly lucky to be dating such a sweet guy.

Sam angled his head to one side. "Are you okay? You seem a bit ... down."

"I'm worried about the festival." I explained how I'd

been so sure that Aaron was the killer but realized I was wrong. And I told him Aaron's theory about Madison. "But I'm not sure I see her as the killer. She and Zoe both seem like nice people."

"Let's think…" Sam ran a hand over his chin. "Did you ever hear back from Alice with any information about Tiffany? Or hear if Zeke had a chance to talk to Kayla to confirm Madison and Zoe's alibis?"

I shook my head and reached in my purse. "I'll text them both again."

I sent off two messages but got no reply.

Sam rubbed Bella's tummy as she twisted on her back on the entryway rug, then he turned to me. "Let's go ahead and eat. Maybe by the time we're done, we will have heard from Alice or Zeke."

"Sounds like a good idea." I followed him into the kitchen, inhaled deeply, and peeked in the oven. Yep, I was right. Those were tortilla chips I smelled warming up. "What can I do to help?"

"Is eating on the patio okay with you?"

The sun was sinking toward the horizon, but we had at least another hour of daylight left, and Sam had such a nice patio. I readily agreed and slipped on my jacket, and Sam sent me out to set the table. As soon as I walked out the kitchen door, my breath caught in my chest, and I stopped.

When my grandparents lived at Ashlington, my parents, brother, and I visited at Thanksgiving or Christmas each year and often came for several days in the summer. Last year, I first went to Sam's house after I moved to Dogwood Springs in June. I'd never been to Ashlington in early May. Now I understood where Great-Great-Grandma Elsie had gotten her inspiration to fill the town with dogwood trees.

Near the house, carefully worked into the recent landscaping, clusters of white dogwoods shone in the setting sun. And beyond the backyard, the rolling Ozark hills alternated in squares of fields and woods dotted with bursts of white. No wonder my ancestors had chosen this ridge as the setting for their home. It was the most restful, beautiful view I could imagine. The longer I gazed at it, feeling the light breeze and listening to the soft hum of insects, the more a sense of peace soaked through me.

Eventually, when Sam passed me carrying a large foil pan covered in bubbling cheese, I drew myself back to thoughts of dinner, and I set the outdoor table. Soon the two of us were seated, and Bella stood beside the table, eagerly eating the kibble and canned food I'd packed for her. Sam and I filled our plates, and I thanked him for getting all my favorites—chicken enchiladas, rice, beans, and chips with salsa and queso.

We'd barely lifted our forks when his phone beeped.

He pulled it from his pocket. "I should take this." He gestured to the table. "Please, eat." He wandered into his backyard, talking quietly into his phone.

For a while I sat there, wanting to be polite and wait for him, despite what he'd said.

But the call went on and on. From the bits I overheard,

it sounded like he was perhaps talking with a potential grad student with lots of questions. Eventually, I began eating.

Maybe it was the view, but despite my stress over the fact that the festival started the next morning, and the murderer was still at large, once I tasted the gooey goodness of melted cheese and the spicy meat of the chicken enchiladas and sampled the crunchy chips dipped in salsa and queso, I was hungry.

By the time Sam started walking back toward me, Bella was investigating the yard, and I'd already eaten an enchilada, a good-sized portion of both rice and beans, and more chips and queso than I'd care to admit. Hopefully, the chip bowl didn't look more than half empty.

"I'll write up an official offer tomorrow and email it to you," Sam said into the phone. "I'm thrilled you're going to be joining my team." He slid the phone back in his pocket and sat back down. "Sorry about that."

"Is everything all good?" I asked.

"Everything's great." He grinned and scooped two enchiladas onto his plate. "Except that I'm starving. Since we're outside, you wouldn't think I'd smell the food, but the whole time I was on the phone, I kept catching a whiff of these chips." He took one, scooped it full of salsa, and ate it.

"It's because you heated them," I said. "Which makes them even more yummy, so thank you."

We talked a long while, catching up on the rest of our lives, and finishing our dinner.

Once we took our plates back to the kitchen, Sam

brought out two cartons of Minnesota's Pride ice cream, his favorite dessert, which he had served me almost every time I'd been at his house. Today he offered me a choice of Cherry Chocolate Chunk and Blackberry Crumble Swirl.

I opted for the blackberry, and he had a big scoop of each. We took our bowls back to the porch and returned to the topic of the two recent murders.

"Tell me more about your conversation with Aaron," Sam said. "You feel confident he's not the killer?"

"I do." I scooped up a bite of ice cream and looked back up at Sam. "Of course, I felt confident after I talked with Madison and Zoe that they were innocent too, but now I'm not so sure about Madison."

"Maybe we'll hear something soon that will—"

My phone rang from inside my jacket pocket, and I pulled it out. "It's Cleo."

Sam sat up taller.

I answered the call. "Hi, Cleo. I'm having dinner with Sam. What have you got?"

"Put me on speaker," she said. "He should hear this too."

I did as she asked. "Okay, go ahead."

"I talked with a friend of mine," Cleo said. "She's a couple of years older than me, the same age as Madison. What Aaron heard was correct. Apparently, Madison hated Darcy because"—Cleo paused dramatically—"when Madison was a senior and Darcy was a sophomore, Darcy beat her out for Dogwood Queen."

"Ooh," I said. "Very interesting."

"There's more. My friend told me that Madison always

talked like if she'd won the queen title, she might have also won Bryce's affection. She had a real thing for him in high school, even though she was two years older."

So Darcy, Cleo, *and* Madison all had a thing for Bryce? "Was everybody in love with this guy in high school?" I asked.

"He was—and still is—a really good guy," Cleo said defensively. "But there's more. Madison married right out of high school and immediately got pregnant with Zoe. My friend thinks that after Darcy and her husband got divorced and she started working for Bryce as a receptionist, she might have gotten interested in him again."

Sam laid his spoon in his bowl. "So you're saying Madison might have killed Darcy not only because she thought her daughter was unfairly eliminated from the queen contest, but also because Darcy beat her out years ago when she was a candidate herself?"

"Yep," Cleo said. "Maybe even because she wanted Darcy out of the picture so she could have Bryce for herself today."

Sam's forehead creased. "That does add up to a lot of motive."

"That's what I thought," Cleo said.

"Madison could very well be the killer," I said.

Sam nodded. "It sure is looking that way. And—

Cleo gasped.

"What's wrong?" Sam and I said in unison.

"I just got a text from Zeke," Cleo said.

A half second later, a text appeared on my screen, and Sam's phone dinged in his pocket.

I read the brief message, and my stomach tightened. "We both got it too," I told Cleo.

Then I held my phone out to Sam so he could read Zeke's message.

*ZOE'S MISSING!!!*

## Chapter Eighteen

SAM WHIPPED OUT HIS PHONE. "Tell Zeke I'm setting up a conference call with Cleo and Alice."

I quickly typed in his message.

Sam put his phone on speaker and sat it on the table between us. Soon the five of us were on the line together.

"Tell us what you know, Zeke," Cleo said.

"Okay." He spoke faster than normal, his words clipped. "About six, Zoe's mom called me, wanting to know if I'd seen her. At five, they were both at the vet clinic. Zoe rides her bike there after school and works for an hour or so. Normally, she puts her bike in her mom's hatchback and rides home with her, but today her mom had to buy groceries."

"So she rode her bike home?" Alice asked.

"She was supposed to," Zeke said. "But when her mom got home, Zoe wasn't there, and she wasn't answering her phone."

"She could have had a bike wreck," Cleo said.

"Her mom thought that, and she went back and drove the route Zoe would have taken," Zeke said.

Sam looked over at me. "Maybe she went to a friend's house."

"Mrs. Thompson called all of Zoe's good friends," Zeke said. "Nobody's seen or heard from her."

"It's a quarter of eight," Alice said gently. "She's only been missing about three hours. I know that with what has gone on in town, it does sound alarming that no one's heard from her. But there were times when my daughter was in her teens, that she, um..." Alice paused. "Needed a break from me. Maybe Zoe went to a park to walk around?"

"I can see her needing a break from her mom," Zeke admitted. "But why hasn't anyone else heard from her? And why isn't she answering texts?"

I shot an uneasy glance at Sam. That did sound bad. "Has, um, has her mom called the police? I know Zoe's not considered a missing person yet, but with what has been going on..."

"I talked with Mrs. Thompson right before I contacted you guys," Zeke said. "She's probably on the phone with the cops right now. But whoever the murderer is, they've already killed two people. What if ... what if..." His voice cracked, and he stopped.

My mind raced, trying to find a way to help. "Zeke, if Zoe knew something about who the murderer was, would she have told you?"

"Oh, yeah," he replied. His voice was a little stronger but

still not normal. "We talked about it almost the whole lunch period."

"And...?"

"She didn't say anything," Zeke said.

That was a positive. Maybe this was all teenage drama.

"I'll keep texting more of her friends," Zeke said. "Maybe I'll find her."

"If her mom is telling the police, checking with her friends seems like the best thing you can do to help," I said. "Keep us posted, okay?"

Zeke promised he would text the minute he heard anything, no matter what time it was.

Sam hung up. "Do you think she's okay?"

"I don't know. I hope so, but I keep wondering if maybe the killer isn't Madison, maybe we've missed something, and they've struck again. What if the killer thought Zoe saw something or knew something? What if Zoe's body, like Darcy and Cameron's, is at the fairgrounds? Do you think I should—?"

"Go wander around there in the dark and see if you can end up dead as well?" Sam's eyebrows pinched inward, and he stared at me. "Don't they have overnight security at the fairgrounds since all the vendors have set up their tents?"

I sat up taller, "Yeah, they do. There's a group of volunteers who start patrolling the grounds as soon as it gets dark tonight."

"Do you know the number of any of them?"

I nodded.

"Why don't you call them," Sam said. "Tell them a girl is missing, so they can be on the lookout."

"Okay," I scrolled through numbers on my phone until I found a guy who I knew was on security patrol for the first part of the night and called him. I still felt like I should do more, but at least it was something.

I stayed at Sam's for about half an hour more, then headed home. With all the interruptions, Sam said we hadn't had much of a date night, but he promised to make it up to me soon.

Even after I got back to my apartment, though, I hadn't heard any more from Zeke, which meant Zoe was still missing.

I went to bed and tried to tell myself I'd responded in a reasonable fashion and that Sam was right—my plan to scour the fairgrounds in the dark with a killer on the loose was a bad idea—but I tossed and turned for hours.

What if Zoe had been killed?

In the middle of the night, I jolted awake. Had my phone dinged with a text telling me Zoe was found?

I climbed out of bed and, in the dim light coming through the curtains, found my phone on the dresser.

It showed that it was three thirty-seven, but there was no message at the top of the screen. I opened the messaging app to see if maybe my notifications settings were wrong.

Even in the app, there was no new message from Zeke.

Not a word, even though he had promised to be in touch no matter what time he heard news about Zoe.

Maybe Bella made a noise in her sleep and that was what woke me.

Wait a minute. Maybe Zeke thought he shouldn't text adults in the middle of the night. Everyone I knew under thirty always had their phone on silent, but someone like Alice might not. Maybe Zeke didn't want to wake her and had used email.

I climbed back under the covers with my phone, and the bed squeaked.

Over in her cushy doggy bed in the corner of my bedroom, Bella raised her head.

"It's not morning yet," I said. "Go back to sleep."

She laid her head back down, wriggled a bit, and then was still.

I laid on my back, buried my head under the covers, and in my warm, dark tent, propped up the phone on my bent knees. Then I opened my email.

Spam, spam, something from Rodney, and an offer for a free coffee or tea at the Dogwood Café.

Nothing from Zeke.

Could he have heard she was okay and forgotten to text us?

Nope. Not Zeke. He was too on the ball and, from every-thing I saw, Zoe mattered too much to him.

Which meant she'd been missing for almost eleven hours, long past the time she was expected home, long past the point where any teenager would have checked their phone. Madison had to be out of her mind with worry, and Zeke as well.

By this point, even though Zoe officially hadn't been gone long enough to be considered a missing person, I was sure Detective Harper had officers out looking for her.

Because it was bad enough that Darcy and Cameron had been killed, but if the town lost a high school girl as well, it would be even more tragic.

There was, of course, one other possibility, one I hadn't wanted to mention to Zeke. It could be that Zoe was the murderer and that she'd run away because she was afraid that she might get caught.

Oh, I hated to even consider that Zeke might have been dating a murderer. But Zoe had a motive for killing Darcy. She might have been more upset about being cut from the queen contest than she let on. And she had seemed really uneasy when I talked with her and Madison about that day at the fairgrounds.

And, just like our other suspects, she could have killed Cameron because he saw something that made him suspect her.

Aargh. All the options were horrible. Either Zoe was in danger, she'd killed two people, or she was already dead. I'd been successful in the past, solving mysteries. Why was this one so hard to figure out?

But what could I do in the middle of the night? I'd told Sam I wouldn't go to the fairgrounds at night, but I certainly wasn't going back to sleep.

Frustrated, I scanned through my emails once more and

opened the message from Rodney. He'd sent it in the afternoon, about the time I'd been talking with Eileen about the key. Things had been so busy since that I hadn't seen the message.

*Libby,*

*You got a call about the girl in the painting, Ivy Whitfield. Someone knows who she is.*

My heart rate sped.

With all that was going on, I'd forgotten all about Ivy. Wouldn't it be cool if Sam and I could learn where she went when she left the area and how her life turned out?

I kept reading.

*Unfortunately, the phone message was taken by the new volunteer, Andrea.*

Uh-oh. We were incredibly grateful to anyone willing to help out at the museum, but some volunteers were better at specific tasks. Andrea, a woman in her forties, never should have been answering the phone. Her mind was sharp but seemed to go in a thousand different directions at once. Sometimes she'd even ask a question and appear to start thinking of something else halfway through your answer.

*Andrea wrote down that "this person" knows who Ivy is, but she didn't get a number or a name.*

*—Rodney*

I jabbed at the phone to close the email and thought for a moment.

Even with the landline, there had to be a record of calls that had come in. The only problem was that I had no idea how to access it.

Double aargh.

And then, as if I didn't have enough to worry about in the middle of the night, an odd thought popped into my head.

When Sam was on the phone during our dinner on the patio at Ashlington, why did he say that he'd type up an offer and send it out? Wouldn't a staff member in graduate studies or some such office send an offer of a research position or stipend to a potential grad student? Why would Sam say that he, personally, would type it?

Unless, of course, he hadn't been talking to a potential grad student.

Maybe the call was about something else entirely.

Maybe Sam was hiring someone for a company like the one he ran out west.

I drew in an uneasy breath. He hadn't mentioned anything about starting a company. Oh, I could certainly imagine that someone who had run a huge tech firm in California might get bored with teaching. He might want more excitement and more challenges. Nine-figure deals and wheeling and dealing. But...

Why hadn't he mentioned it to me?

Suddenly, a really bad, really paranoid thought flitted through my head—the kind of thought that only came to mind in the middle of the night.

What if Sam hadn't mentioned his plan for a business because he wasn't just bored with teaching? What if he was also bored with Dogwood Springs and bored with me? What if he was moving back to California? What if, like my ex-husband, he was ready to move on to someone else? Had I been wrong to trust, wrong to take a chance with another man?

I put my phone on the nightstand, turned over my pillow, and jabbed at it with my fist.

Finally, after weeks without progress, we had a lead on Ivy Whitfield, only to have it bungled by a certain volunteer. A year and a half after my divorce, I thought I was past my ex-husband's betrayal enough to trust another man, only to have paranoia buzzing in my brain like a blood-thirsty mosquito.

And—by far, the worst of all—Zoe was still missing.

## Chapter Nineteen

AT A QUARTER 'TIL FIVE, I got out of bed, turned on the light, and rummaged around in my closet.

Bella opened one eye and tipped her head at me.

"Yeah, I know it's still dark, girl. But I can't lay here, worrying about Zoe and not doing anything, any longer. Besides, I have a plan."

Bella trotted over to me and rubbed her head against the leg of my pajamas.

"Of course, you can come." I ran a hand over her soft fur. "First, though, I'll turn on the light by my back door and let you out, then I'll fix you an early breakfast."

At the word breakfast, Bella's ears perked up.

I padded to the kitchen in my slippers and let her out, allowing a gust of wind to swirl into my kitchen.

Later in the day, it would probably be beautiful outside. Now, while it was still dark, the temperature was rather chilly.

But those cool temperatures weren't going to stop me. What we needed, if we were going to figure out what happened to Zoe, was to learn who killed Darcy and Cameron. Our best hope, at this point, was to find some piece of physical evidence that the police missed at one of the two crime scenes.

Darcy's murder scene, the area by the waterfall, had been exposed to rain as well as several days of festival volunteers and vendors wandering over to speculate on what had happened. Even if I found some bit of physical evidence near the waterfall, I couldn't know it had been left there at the time of the murder. But Cameron had been killed less than two days ago, on Wednesday night. The police had collected evidence, two people from Eileen's restaurant had cleaned the truck, and the rest of the time, it had been locked up.

Granted, the chance was small that physical evidence from the murder remained after the police had searched the truck and Eileen's staff had cleaned it. But what if they missed something? What if a vital clue was just sitting there?

For a moment, I toyed with my phone. If I wanted to be extra cautious, I could text Cleo or Sam and see if, like me, they were awake, worrying about Zoe. If they were, they could join me on my sleuthing mission at the food truck.

Sam was probably sound asleep. In the past, when we'd made plans on Saturdays, I'd learned that he was not by nature an early riser. And Cleo?

I leaned against the kitchen counter, watching Bella out the window and listening intently.

Nope. I didn't hear a sound upstairs.

If I texted either of them, I'd wake them up. Which meant I should take care of this bit of sleuthing on my own.

After all, I wouldn't be questioning a suspect, simply looking for clues. Some vendors, especially ones with large displays to arrange, might arrive at the fairgrounds extra early. The volunteer team would be patrolling, available to come if I called. And I'd have Bella with me.

As if on cue, Bella trotted back to the door.

I let her in before she had a chance to bark and wake Cleo.

Once Bella's food bowl was filled, I ate some cereal. Then I hopped in the shower, dressed in dark colors, and put on my tennis shoes and a heavy jacket. I dearly loved my oversized purse, but it was too much to haul along when I was looking for clues. I slid my keys in one of my jacket pockets. I'd leave my purse in my trunk.

I grabbed Bella's leash and added two more items to my jacket pockets—my pepper spray and the key to the Pit & Pickle food truck.

It was a long shot, but if I went through that truck, I might find a clue that would link the killer to Cameron's murder.

～

Even with all the tourists in town for the festival, at five thirty on a Friday morning, Dogwood Springs was asleep. I only saw two cars on my way to the fairgrounds, both headed the opposite direction down Hartley Road.

By the time I'd parked in the lot near the stage, it was still mostly dark, but a faint, rosy glow hovered on the eastern horizon. As I stepped out of the car, the wind had died down, the temperature had warmed up a degree or two, and a chorus of bird songs filled the air, sounding far too happy for a time when a teenage girl was missing. I let Bella out of the car and listened for sounds of people in the park.

I knew there had to be out-of-town vendors like Jimbo parked in the main lot. And I knew four volunteers should be on patrol. But I didn't see or hear anyone.

I leaned down and spoke near Bella's ear as I clipped on her leash. "Okay, girl, we need to be very quiet. If there is a killer around the fairgrounds, I want to check out that food truck and get back home before they notice we're here." Maybe I'd quickly find a clue and be back home in time to have another cup of tea before I had to return to work all day at the museum's tent.

Although frankly, I wouldn't be surprised if, given the fact that Zoe was still missing, the police canceled the festival entirely. Zoe's disappearance had to drive an enormous hole into Detective Harper's theory that Bryce was the killer. Bryce was in custody.

If I found a clue that led to the real killer, not only might it help the police determine what happened to Zoe, it also might lead to an arrest that would mean the festival could go ahead without fear of another murder.

I ran a hand over the soft fur on Bella's head—more to ease my own nervousness than to comfort her—and whispered near her ear, "Let's go."

I wouldn't have ventured across an unfamiliar field, where I might trip over something or step in a hole, without a flashlight. But there was enough light that, at least here in the parking lot where I'd walked many times before, Bella and I could pick our way along.

As we neared the smaller vendor area, Bella found an empty single-serving potato chip bag on the ground. She would have gladly stayed there, sniffing it, for hours, but I led her on. Soon we crept down the wide gravel path that separated the two vendor areas and ran in front of the museum's tent and the Pit & Pickle truck.

Yesterday, the food truck had been silent, but now its generator was humming. Sometime after I left, one of Eileen's staff members must have come by and switched it on to cool down the refrigerator.

I walked around to the back of the truck and glanced toward the museum's tent. All looked well, although Aaron hadn't yet tied the red flags to the rope that ran from the far, back corner of the canopy to the soft pretzel truck.

I slid the key to the food truck out of my jacket pocket. Then I unlocked the back door, urged Bella inside, and quickly followed her in and closed the door behind us.

Inside, the smell of disinfectant was so strong that I almost sneezed, and Bella wrinkled up her nose. And now that we were out of the breeze, my heavy jacket was far too hot. I slipped it off and hung it on a hook near the door.

I had a fleeting thought that dogs probably weren't allowed in commercial kitchen space, but shook my head, forcing myself to focus. Health violations were the least of our worries if the murderer didn't get caught. I made a silent promise to myself to offer to come scrub the floor of the truck.

But it was too dark in here to look for clues. I turned on the flashlight app on my phone.

When I'd been in the food truck with Cleo, I'd only gotten a glimpse before we found Cameron's body. This time, Bella sniffed this way and that, and I looked at everything closely.

The space inside the truck was tightly packed, and every surface—from the oven, range, and griddle to the fryers, fridge, sink, and countertops—was stainless steel, all of it sleek and gleaming.

I had pictured a doorway leading from the food prep area to the cab of the truck, but, except for a small window, the wall behind the cab was solid, filled with a hot water heater and a sink. There was nowhere to sit down, and workspace was tight. Two, at most three, people could possibly work here at once.

Tight as it was, Eileen's staff seemed to have everything ready for making funnel cakes. A countertop near the sink held huge bags of flour and powdered sugar and enormous bottles of cooking oil.

Magnets held laminated recipes for traditional vanilla

and chocolate funnel cake batter to the metal cabinet doors, as well as a list of measurements to be used with toppings.

I was just envisioning a traditional funnel cake topped with cold strawberry sauce and whipped cream when I heard a *clunk* directly overhead.

My breath froze in my lungs.

I pressed my phone against my jeans to cover the hole where the light came out and hunkered down below the level of the window to the truck's cab, silent.

Somewhere nearby, a squirrel chittered, and then tiny feet skittered above me.

My heart sped. Squirrels were Bella's personal nemesis. She felt duty-bound to warn everyone within earshot whenever she spotted one, and it seemed that one had jumped from a nearby tree onto the top of the food truck.

"Please, please, don't bark," I whispered to her. If the killer was nearby, I didn't want them to find me.

In the dim light from the window to the cab area, I saw her tilt her head at me, but she remained silent.

I let out an enormous exhale and hugged her. "Thank you. Good girl. Good girl, Bella," I whispered, and I scratched her ears.

It was odd, though. There had been times when we were walking on Elm Street when she barked no matter what I said. Was she smart enough to sense the fear in my voice?

Either way, I didn't hear any more squirrels. "Okay, let's get back to work. We're looking for a clue that might tell us who was here the night Cameron was killed."

Bella sniffed at the refrigerator door.

That wasn't very helpful, as I didn't think the killer had opened the fridge while they were killing Cameron. No matter how smart Bella was, though, she was still a dog. She could be distracted from almost anything with food.

I scanned the work surfaces, even shifted each bag of flour and powdered sugar, but found nothing on the countertops.

Eventually, Bella seemed so interested in the fridge that I opened the door. Cool air flowed out, but the inside was completely empty, perhaps due to be loaded with fresh milk and other supplies closer to opening time. A strong aroma of barbecue lingered in the fridge, so I understood why she was intrigued.

"All that's left to check is the floor, girl." I started in one corner, moving my flashlight beam in a slow sweeping motion. Other than slightly muddy footprints that matched my tennis shoes and Bella's paws, I found nothing.

I heard a soft *clunk* and glanced above me.

That squirrel again.

And Bella was still over near the fridge.

"There's no barbecue left in there, Bella," I whispered. "It's empty."

She let out a soft whine.

"I know it's disappointing, but—"

She whined again and pawed at the floor.

And that's when the beam of my flashlight glinted off something gold wedged in the crack between the flooring and the wall. Was it an earring?

*No.*

I bent down and picked up a small piece of gold-colored metal shaped like a letter B.

*Harry's zipper pull.*

As I stood and stared at it, things began to click in my brain.

Alice had thought Harry was in his car in the Pit & Pickle parking lot.

Just like how last night, when I got to Ashlington, I'd thought someone was in Sam's office with him.

But both Alice and I had only heard a voice, and a voice could be transmitted electronically, even recorded and played back.

If Jimbo had lied, and Harry had killed Darcy, Harry would be sure to set up a solid alibi before he killed again. All he needed was a partner, someone to sit in his car and play a recording of him talking, again and again.

But why? Why would Harry kill Darcy? I had no idea, but I did have hard evidence. It was time to talk to Detective Harper.

I turned, ready to hurry home and call him. Maybe the two of us could figure it out and—

The back door to the food truck creaked open.

## Chapter Twenty

MY HEART POUNDED as I spun around.

"Oh, it's you." Harry climbed up into the truck, pointing a flashlight right at me.

My mind raced, desperate for a way to appear nonchalant, and I planted a hand dramatically on my chest. "You nearly scared me to death." I gestured for him to lower his flashlight, which had a beam about four times as bright as the flashlight on my phone.

Unfortunately, his flashlight wasn't just bright. It was one of those long, heavy metal models that looked like it could double as a weapon.

"Here." He switched on the overhead light and turned off his flashlight. "I didn't mean to frighten you. I saw a light in here, and I was afraid someone was stealing Eileen's supplies."

"Nope. Just me." I slid the gold zipper pull into my

pocket, trying to be discreet. So far, it seemed he had no idea I suspected him. "What are you doing here this early, Harry?"

He shrugged and waved a hand to one side. "I get up at five every morning, even if I don't set an alarm. What about you?"

Something about his gesture clicked in my brain. It was the same hand motion he'd made when he tried to pick up a takeout order for someone named Jack at the Pit & Pickle.

And then, like a massive, rogue wave crashing into an unsuspecting wader, it hit me. Everything suddenly made sense.

Harry answering when a different name was called for a takeout order.

Local vendors, like Imani's husband, losing their premium festival locations.

And Darcy, the steering committee member who best understood finance and accounting, as the first murder victim.

Harry, who acted so charming, so generous with his time for running the festival, wasn't at all what he appeared. He was running a scam, and he had killed Darcy and Cameron.

And I still hadn't answered his question about why I was here. "Uh, uh, I'm checking on things for Eileen, and up early, nervous about the big day, I guess. But all is well." I gave the most confident smile I could muster. "I'd better run home and get some breakfast before I have to be back here before the festival opens at nine."

The twinkle in Harry's blue eyes shifted to a hard gleam, and he gave me a look of pity. "Libby, you have to be the world's worst liar." He stepped closer. "You won't be going home for breakfast. You won't be going to the police with that zipper pull. In fact, you won't be going anywhere. You'll be dead."

I drew in a deep breath and opened my mouth to—

"Don't bother screaming. I sent the volunteers who were patrolling the fairgrounds home as soon as I arrived this morning. No one's started setting up yet today. And if any of the vendors camping in the main parking lot are awake, they won't get here fast enough to save you."

Bella moved closer to my side.

My pulse raced, and I reached for my pepper spray—

Which was zipped in one of the pockets of my jacket, hanging on a hook near the door.

Why, oh why, hadn't I left my jacket on? Or been smart enough to transfer the pepper spray to the pocket of my jeans? Or locked the door of the truck behind me once I was inside?

I'd been stupid, stupid, stupid, thinking I was safe. To get to the pepper spray, I'd have to go past Harry, fumble around with my jacket until I found the right pocket, and then unzip it.

How could I have made such a mistake?

Harry blocked the only exit, he was bigger than me, and he was going to kill me, right here in the Pit & Pickle food truck where he'd killed Cameron, probably by bashing me in the head with that big flashlight. He'd take the zipper pull I found, wipe away any fingerprints he left, and no one would know he was the murderer.

But one thing confused me. If Zoe had suspected Harry, she would have told Zeke. And if she didn't know what Harry was up to, why would he have killed her? "What about Zoe? Is she okay?"

"Zoe?" Harry's eyes narrowed. "Zoe Thompson, the queen candidate?"

I nodded.

"I have no idea. I didn't do anything to her. I'd never hurt a kid." His voice rang with indignation as if I'd offended his sense of honor.

Such as it was, given that he was a murderer.

"Really," he said. "I was only in this for the money."

One good thing, at least. If Harry didn't kill her, Zoe was probably safe.

Unlike me.

Unless I could stall long enough to come up with a way out of this trailer. I met his eyes and tried to keep my voice from shaking. "If you're going to kill me, at least satisfy my curiosity. What, uh, what was it?" I asked. "Some kind of kickback deal you and your partner had for giving the out-of-town vendors the best spots?"

Harry's eyebrows raised as if he was impressed with all that I'd figured out. "I guess it can't hurt to tell you. It's more than that. By the time anyone realizes I'm gone, the festival account will be drained. Granted, it's not as big a haul as I'd get if I had the gate proceeds from the entire festival, but I'll get all the vendor fees, those kickbacks, and the money from ticket preorders."

Heat flushed through my whole body. Wasn't killing two people—uh, three, counting me—in Dogwood Springs enough? Did he also have to take the money for the Good Neighbor Fund? He was literally stealing money from children in need.

I thought of how he'd accidentally answered to a different name, and I glared at him. "I bet you've run this con in other towns. You may have even killed other people."

"I never... Darcy and Cameron were the first... If only she hadn't figured out what I was doing..." He waved his empty hand at me as if to ward off my words. "Enough of this." Then he raised the arm holding the long, metal flashlight and lunged toward me.

Bella barked at top volume, and I darted to one side, sending Harry off-balance.

In that second, I grabbed a bag of powdered sugar, ripped it open, and threw it at him, sending out an enormous white cloud. "Run, Bella!" I cried as I grabbed my jacket from the hook by the door and leapt out of the food truck.

"Nice try, Libby!" Harry yelled as he followed me.

My heart felt like it was going to beat right out of my chest.

Harry was taller than me. His legs were longer. And, despite the fact that he was at least thirty years older, he was so fit that he was probably faster. If I stopped to dig out my pepper spray, could I find the canister and get it out fast enough?

Not likely.

Which meant I had only one hope for escape.

Chapter Twenty-One

ADRENALINE SHOT THROUGH MY VEINS, and I sprinted behind the museum's tent where—for at least a few seconds —I was hidden from view. In that precious window of time, I dodged under the rope Aaron had strung from the corner of the museum's canopy to the pretzel truck behind it. Then I cut through the space between the pretzel truck and the next tent, Bella right beside me, coming out on a pathway one aisle over in the vendor area.

I heard a strangled cry, and the footsteps behind me stopped.

I gasped for breath. At last, I had a moment to prepare myself to fight back. I found the jacket pocket with the pepper spray, unzipped it, grabbed the canister, and started running again.

A second later, footsteps once more pounded behind me. "Who put that rope there?" Harry yelled as he closed in on me. "It nearly strangled me."

I spun, made sure Bella was out of the way, and pressed the button on the pepper spray, pointing it right at his face.

Harry sank to the ground, coughing.

*Yes!*

As fast as I could, I kicked the flashlight out of his hand and grabbed it.

"Keep an eye on him, Bella." I pointed at Harry.

She let out a low growl, then began barking at top volume.

And I dialed 911.

Five minutes later, Harry managed to sit up, but tears streamed from his eyes, his nose was running, and the skin on one cheek, where the bulk of the pepper spray hit him, was red and blistered. Add in the fact that he was coughing violently, and I wasn't concerned for my safety or for his escape.

Bella, who ordinarily seemed concerned whenever someone was in pain, stood right beside me. Either the smell of the pepper spray kept her away or she understood that Harry had wanted to harm me.

A siren wailed in the distance and then drew closer. The louder it grew, the lower Harry's shoulders sank. When Officers Tate and Davis ran up, I explained that Harry had killed both Darcy and Cameron and tried to kill me.

Harry willingly surrendered. "Just get me somewhere that I can wash this stuff off," he begged.

As Officer Davis led him to the restrooms, my shoulders sagged, and my hands started shaking.

As he had before, Officer Tate led me to the museum tent to sit down. "Whenever you're ready, tell me more about what happened."

I nodded, pulled Bella close, and held up my phone. "Can I send a quick text first?"

"Go ahead."

I sent a message to my friends, letting them know that Harry was the killer, that I was all right, and that he claimed—and I believed him—to have nothing to do with Zoe's disappearance. I told them I was answering questions from the police, promised to fill them in on more details later, and slid the phone back in my pocket.

I had just finished explaining all that had happened and giving Officer Tate the zipper pull, which he bagged as evidence, when I heard footsteps coming up behind me and turned.

"Libby, are you okay?" Detective Harper strode toward the museum's tent, looking worse than I'd ever seen him. His eyes were bloodshot, his uniform was rumpled, and his breath was heavy as if he'd been running.

"She's fine, sir. Disabled the assailant with pepper spray." Officer Tate's voice rang with respect.

"Just a little shaky afterward," I said.

"Davis took the suspect to the restrooms to wash off the spray. Libby got him pretty good," Officer Tate said.

I mentally prepared myself for a lecture from Detective

Harper on why I shouldn't be sleuthing, but he seemed more interested in talking with Officer Tate.

After a few more questions, Detective Harper sent Tate to join Officer Davis. "Get Harry cleaned up, and then I want to talk to him." He took Officer Tate's chair and turned to me. "Are you feeling up to giving me a statement?"

I nodded.

Bella edged up next to him and rubbed her head against his leg.

He looked down at her, gave her a quick pat, and focused on me again. "Okay, start at the beginning. Why were you out here at the fairgrounds so early? Something for the steering committee?"

Oh. No wonder he didn't seem mad at me for interfering in his investigation. He didn't know that I had been.

I didn't care. I wasn't going to apologize for what I'd done. "Have you learned what happened to Zoe Thompson?" I asked.

"No. I've been up all night with a team, trying to find her."

My attitude softened. No wonder the detective looked the way he did. He was as concerned for Zoe as I was. "I was so worried about her that I couldn't sleep, and I had a key to the Pit & Pickle food truck that I was supposed to give to an employee today." I explained how Eileen wasn't able to be at the fairgrounds when the vendors' trucks were checked.

Detective Harper nodded.

"I thought if Bella and I looked around the food truck, I might find something that would tell me who the killer was, and if I told you, you might find out what's happened to Zoe."

"The team already went over the truck for evidence," he said. "And then I think Eileen's staff cleaned it."

"It was a long shot, but it worked." I told him about the zipper pull Bella had found.

Detective Harper's eyes widened. "Bella found the clue?"

"She sure did." I wrapped an arm around her, leaned down, and gave her a squeeze.

She wriggled free and licked my cheek.

"I shouldn't be surprised," Detective Harper said. "She's better at finding clues than some folks on the force." He shook his head. "But how did Harry know what you were doing?"

"Just my bad luck. He's an early riser and was at the fairgrounds, checking on things. He saw the light from my phone in the food truck and came to see what was going on. He walked in right after I found the zipper pull. And"—I squirmed, reluctant to admit how transparent I'd been—"when he looked at me, he could tell I suspected him."

Detective Harper dipped his chin in acknowledgment.

Did everyone think I was easy to read? I blew out a frustrated breath and told myself that maybe it was just part of who I was. At least I'd been clever enough and lucky enough to escape.

"Once he decided to kill me, he admitted he'd killed Darcy and Cameron," I said. "I guess he figured I wouldn't be telling anyone."

"What about Zoe?" The detective's shoulders tightened, and his voice was filled with dread.

"He adamantly denied having anything to do with her disappearance."

Tension drained from the detective's body. "Thank God."

I explained about Harry's plan to steal the festival proceeds, my theory that he had a partner, and my deduction that he'd run this con before.

At the word *con*, Detective Harper's eyes lit up. "I wonder…"

"What?"

"Harry might be in on the other cons that have been happening around Dogwood Springs, the elderly people who've been persuaded to invest in schemes that are supposed to be guaranteed winners."

"I wouldn't be surprised," I said. "If he's willing to steal funds raised to help children in need, he probably wouldn't have any qualms about taking money from the elderly."

"My thoughts exactly." Detective Harper stood. "I'll get his statement and get back to looking for Zoe." He started to say something else, then stopped. "I still don't like you snooping, Libby, but this one time I understand. The whole force is worried about Zoe. But I sure am glad you had the pepper spray."

"Me too. Will the festival go on?"

"I don't know of any connection between Zoe's disappearance and the festival, so I see no reason to stop it." He glanced over at me. "You're free to go."

Inside my jacket pocket, my phone dinged with one text,

then another, coming in as fast as raindrops in a downpour. I pulled it from my pocket.

I read the messages, and a light, airy feeling filled my chest. "It's Zeke, Zoe's boyfriend," I told the detective. "He says she's safe. She's been safe the whole time."

Detective Harper sank back into his chair. Lines smoothed on his forehead, and he spoke into his radio. "Get someone over to Zeke Anderson's house. He's heard from Zoe. That's the Andersons on Riverbend Drive."

Bella gave a loud, happy bark, and in that instant, the sun rose over the tree line.

A bird began singing nearby, and a ray of sunshine filled the tent, bathing Bella in a golden glow. I leaned down and hugged her to my side, resting my head against hers.

"I'm so happy you're okay!" Imani wrapped me in a tight hug as soon as I stepped into the museum's tent.

"I'm fine. I'm sorry I'm late." I unhooked Bella's leash and pointed to a corner in the back where she could lie down. "I know it's after nine thirty, but I had to run home to change into my steering committee T-shirt and redo my hair and makeup."

"Really? Gee, it's hard to believe you didn't look perfect after catching a double murderer," Imani teased. "Seriously, if it wasn't for you, I bet the whole festival would have been canceled."

I glanced down. It wasn't like I'd established world peace. "How have things been?"

"Fabulous." She gestured toward the crowd that was wandering from tent to tent. "This is the only time since I got here that someone hasn't been here, looking at the displays." She gestured to the three mystery antiques. "People love these and—"

A group of four older women walked up to the tent. "I want to guess the antiques," said one with snow-white hair. "I bet I get them all right."

Her friends cheered her on as she looked at each item and wrote down her answers. She folded her paper into quarters and handed it to Imani, who was holding the glass jar where we were collecting entries.

"If you're a winner, we'll contact you early next week," I said. "If you don't hear from us, be sure to stop by the museum or check on the website to find out what the mystery items were."

The woman nodded, and walked away with her friends, assuring them that she'd guessed every item correctly.

When she had moved well away, I nudged Imani. "Did she get them all?"

Imani unfolded the paper. "She guessed the butter mold with the cow design that Rodney contributed, and she got the hosiery gloves that I put in the game."

"Those gloves have stumped a lot of people. But they were popular at one time, when women wore them to avoid running their stockings while they put them on."

Imani looked back at the woman's answers and giggled.

"She was totally off on the chamber pot you put in the game. She thought it was a serving dish."

I began laughing as well. Maybe it was leftover stress or maybe it was the vision of how a Victorian-era woman would have reacted to the idea of serving food in a chamber pot, but we both got so tickled that we had to sit down to catch our breath.

"Libby," Sylvia walked up to the tent holding a clipboard. "Thank you so much for catching the killer."

"Are you...?" I stood and pointed to the clipboard.

"I'm back as director." Sylvia's voice rang with pride. "I have to say, I was surprised when four steering committee members each called me this morning, begging me to come back. I understand the festival needed someone in charge, but everyone's attitude is so different now."

"I'm not surprised at all," I said. "You ran things fairly, doing your best for the town and its children for years. People know they can trust you."

"Thanks." Sylvia blushed. "I'm not taking it for granted, though. I'm looking at this as a second chance, and I'm going to do a much better job of explaining why things should be done in a certain way. It all seemed so obvious to me, but maybe when I insisted on things without explaining, people saw me as controlling. I'm not, really..." She laughed. "Well, maybe I am a little controlling, but only because I know how important the checks and balances of the system are."

"I wouldn't be surprised if you're directing this festival for years to come," I said.

Clearly, it was good for her. The woman looked so invigorated that running a festival could be marketed as better than vitamins.

"You're not the first person who's said that. And I'd love it. I've missed the excitement." Sylvia's phone dinged in her pocket, and she pulled it out. "Whoops. There's a crisis at the gate. Harry didn't get enough change for the start-up till, and they've already run out. Got to go."

She trotted off toward the main parking lot with a spring in her step.

A moment later, I heard a faint cough and turned.

Madison and Zoe Thompson stood beside the mystery antiques.

Bella wriggled out the side of the tent and walked over beside Zoe, rubbing her head against Zoe's jeans so much that I knew they'd be coated in dog hair.

"Zoe!" In spite of the fact that I didn't know her well, I reached across the table and pulled her into a hug. "I'm so glad you're here, safe and sound."

"I'm sorry I scared you, Miss Ballard." Zoe's face was bright red under her freckles. "Zeke told me that you almost got killed trying to figure out what happened to me."

Madison laid a hand on my arm. "Thank you for caring so much about my girl." Tears shone in her eyes, and she blinked rapidly. "She's just fine now. Everything is just fine." She slid an arm around Zoe's waist and pulled her to her side.

Zoe gave her mom a heartfelt smile, then turned to me.

"Mom and I had to stop by the police station, and then she said we should come see you to explain."

Madison nodded, and when Zoe remained silent, cleared her throat.

"Darcy, uh"—Zoe looked down—"Darcy didn't actually eliminate me from the queen finalists. I told her I didn't want to be in the contest. The whole idea of being up there on stage and having everyone looking at me..." She shuddered. "It's not the same as being one girl out of twelve in the color guard. But I knew my mom really, really wanted me to be in the contest, wanted me to win the crown, so I asked Darcy if she could say I didn't make the finals. I didn't want to hurt my mom's feelings and tell her that what mattered so much to her didn't matter to me."

Madison winced. "Then things got complicated. Because when Darcy was killed, I'd left Zoe and Kayla alone in the restroom working on Kayla's shirt." She rocked back and forth on her tennis shoes. "I was sitting over near the stage, checking to see if this guy I met on a dating app had messaged me. With all that went on when we found the body, I forgot I'd stepped out for a bit."

"But I knew Mom wasn't with Kayla and me and didn't have an alibi," Zoe said.

Which was why she looked so uncomfortable when I initially talked with the two of them. She thought her mom had deceived me on purpose.

"After Zeke and I talked about the murder Thursday at lunch, I got to thinking about how much my mom wanted me to be queen and how mad she seemed to be at Darcy after I was 'eliminated.' Plus, I always thought she had a thing for Dr. Bryce."

"Which I don't," Madison said. "At least not these days. I did back in high school. What Zoe thought was me being interested in Bryce was actually me thinking he shouldn't be with Darcy."

"So, then I got worried that my mom might possibly have killed Darcy and then killed Cameron to cover it up." Zoe glanced down. "And I sort of freaked out and ran away."

"Where were you?" I asked.

"A friend of mine is out of town. Her whole family went to a funeral. I knew where they kept a spare key, so I was hanging out at their house."

"That's when Dr. Whiskers made things even more complicated," Madison said.

"Dr. Whiskers?" I pictured the cat at the clinic and felt more confused.

"Before I left the vet's office, I put a note on the counter for my mom, telling her that I was going to stay at a friend's house," Zoe said. "We think Dr. Whiskers knocked it off, and it slid under the filing cabinet."

"He's done it before," Madison said. "Once with a bill that we didn't know about until the supplier called to tell us they couldn't fill our order until we paid for the last shipment."

"After I got to my friend's house," Zoe said, "I plugged in my phone, which was almost out of battery. I watched two movies and then I fell asleep, never knowing that the light switch in the room where I'd plugged in my phone controlled the wall outlet. My phone died, and I didn't realize it until I woke up the next morning and found all the texts."

"I was out of my mind with worry, afraid you'd been murdered." Madison shot a look at Zoe. "And so was the rest of the town, like Libby."

"I know, Mom." Zoe looked at her mom, then at me. "I'm really sorry. I can't believe you nearly got killed because of me."

"I'm fine," I said.

"Even so," Madison said, "Zoe's learned her lesson."

"No more lies." Zoe held up a hand like she was swearing an oath. "Even if the truth hurts someone I love. And my mom's learned hers."

"No more pushing Zoe to live out my dreams. I'm going to try to remember that what was important to me at her age might not be important to her," Madison said. "And the two of us are going to try to communicate better with each other, even when it's hard. We're seeing a counselor to help us get started."

"That's wonderful." I beamed at them both. "Thank you for telling me."

"I thought it was the least we could do," Madison said. "Oh, and one more thing." She glanced over at Zoe.

"Would it be okay if I volunteered at the museum on Saturday afternoons?" Zoe asked. "It's such a great place, and even though I'm going to major in computer science in college, I read a lot of history books, and Zeke's been telling me I should ask. I can't be there every week because some-times in the fall we have band competitions, but…"

Happiness swelled in my chest. Not only was Zoe safe, but her relationship with her mom was on the mend, and I'd found a fellow history enthusiast. "We'd be happy to have you volunteer any time, Zoe. I bet we can even find a way to put your computer skills to use if you'd like."

She clapped her hands together like an excited little kid.

I handed her a form. "Just fill this out and bring it with you the first time you come in."

She tucked it into her back pocket and walked away, happily chatting with her mom.

## Chapter Twenty-Two

LATER THAT DAY, when Imani returned to the museum's tent from her dinner break, Bella and I walked through the bustling fairgrounds to meet Cleo, Sam, Zeke, and Alice in the wine and beer garden. The funnel cake truck, which had been closed earlier, was up and running, and I'd been smelling the delicious aroma so long that I was more than ready for dinner. Lines were long at it and the other food trucks, but people waiting didn't seem to mind. I overheard lots of laughter and several comments about how fun the festival was.

On the way, I ran into Sylvia, who told me that Cameron's stepdaughter, Noelle, would be crowned Dogwood Queen. She wasn't in attendance at the festival because of her stepfather's death, but Sylvia would plan a special reception for her in a month or so when she would be crowned and receive the scholarship.

"That's so nice," I said.

"I'm glad it worked out this way," Sylvia said. "When I told Noelle, she thought I'd juggled things to make her win, but she won fair and square. I'm glad that after the upheaval in their lives of losing Cameron, she and her mom will have something happy to focus on."

I was too. Cameron may not have been the best stepdad, but he had cared about Noelle. Losing him so suddenly and violently would be hard on both her and her mom.

Sylvia rushed off, and I continued on toward the wine and beer garden.

The cover band I'd been eager to hear was on stage, looking like they walked right out of the 1970s, complete with leather-fringed vests, granny glasses, and bell-bottom jeans. They started up a new song, and after about five notes, I recognized it as one of my all-time country rock favorites.

Tapping my hand against my thigh in time with the music, I scanned the beer garden. I quickly spotted my friends, who were sitting at a table piled with all manner of festival food favorites. Cleo had a hot dog and onion rings. Zeke had a fried pork tenderloin sandwich and what I thought were fried pickles. And Alice, who normally ate salads, appeared to be making a meal of fried pralines.

Sam had stopped by the museum's tent as soon as he got off work, but at the time I'd been inundated with tourists. He and I had barely gotten to talk, but he'd asked what I'd like for dinner and gotten us both cheeseburgers, fries, and sodas. "This looks delicious." I slid onto the bench next to him.

Bella left me to make the rounds, greeting each person at the table.

Sam pulled me into a tight hug. "I couldn't really tell you earlier, but I'm so glad you're all right."

I hugged him back, savoring the warmth and comfort of his embrace. Maybe my worries the other night had been the product of a lack of sleep.

Then I looked around the table, at my friends, who were each murmuring about how worried they'd been. I was so lucky to have moved to Dogwood Springs when I needed to create a new life for myself, so lucky to have found this group of friends who truly cared about me.

Alice licked some caramel off her finger. "I can't believe Harry was the killer."

"I can't believe you didn't ask me to go to the fairgrounds with you," Cleo said indignantly.

"I thought you were asleep. I didn't want to wake you, and I thought I'd be safe."

She rolled her eyes. "I could have gotten up. If you ever go sleuthing again, you'd better take me with you."

"Hopefully there won't be any more murders in Dogwood Springs, but if there is one, I promise," I told her.

"Or call me," Sam said. "And I sure am glad you had that pepper spray."

Bella nuzzled her way between Zeke and Sam, who scratched between her ears and told her how proud he was of her for finding the clue in the food truck.

I'd already fed her, but when she came back to my side, I gave her one of JoBeth's homemade dog treats.

The music ended, and the lead singer walked to the front of the stage. "We're taking a short break," he told the crowd. "We'll be back as soon as we get a chance to eat some more of those deep-fried pralines. Those things are addictive."

A ripple of laughter flowed through the audience, and people began chatting.

Alice wiped her fingers on a napkin. "Then this is the perfect time for you to explain how you figured out that Harry was the killer, Libby."

"Sure." I set down my cheeseburger and thought back to where it all began. "Even though I didn't realize it at the time, the first clue was when Imani's husband didn't get the same spot for his tent as last year. When I thought about all that had happened in the light of Harry not being honest, I realized that out-of-town vendors might have been paying Harry kickbacks for those premium spots."

Alice's eyes widened, and she slowly nodded.

"After all, who's got more chance of selling food?" I pointed toward the closest vendors. "Someone right along that row, here beside the wine and beer garden and the stage? Or a vendor way on the other side by the portable restrooms?"

"These guys." Alice angled her head toward the vendors nearby. "Unless, of course, it's the only food truck selling deep-fried pralines." She shook her head and looked at the empty paper basket in front of her. "I'll probably gain five pounds from how many I ate tonight. It's a good thing I can only get them a couple of times a year."

The rest of us laughed.

"The second clue," I said, "was the fact that Harry encouraged people to do different jobs than they'd done in the past. If someone is new to running the festival, it would be more logical to keep other people in jobs they knew well to make sure things went smoothly. But if Harry had people doing unfamiliar jobs, they were less likely to notice what he was up to."

"Good point," Sam said. "If you take over a company that's doing well, you don't make a lot of changes right away. You wait until you get a picture of how things work."

I took a quick sip of my soda. "Another clue was that Darcy was the first victim. If anyone on the steering committee was going to notice something off financially, it would have been her. She might not have even realized Harry was doing anything illegal when she asked him about irregularities. But if she mentioned something before the photo shoot, he must have realized he had to act quickly."

"He can't have planned to kill her then," Zeke said. "He was taking a real risk with so many people around."

"I know." A chill ran down my spine. "He must have murdered her minutes before he met me. I think Bella even picked up on it. I remember her sniffing at his hands and looking over at me when we first saw him that day."

Cleo hesitated, an onion ring halfway to her mouth. "But I thought he was on the phone at the time of Darcy's murder."

"He had Jimbo lie for him. I guess Jimbo hasn't always been the most law-abiding citizen, and Harry had some dirt on him," I said. "I bet that was why Jimbo was so kind when you and I found Cameron dead, Cleo. He suspected Harry had gotten violent. But when Jimbo heard the sirens coming, his unease around the police surfaced, and he disappeared. Detective Harper told me when he went back to Jimbo today, he said he must have misremembered. He wasn't really on the phone with Harry at the time of Darcy's murder."

Zeke's eyes narrowed. "There must have been more, though, that helped you work it out."

"Yeah, there was. When I looked at it all together, it was logical that Cameron was the second victim. If Darcy suspected something was off with the accounts of the festival, she'd probably discuss it with a fellow banker." I took another drink of my soda.

"Why didn't Cameron go to the cops when Darcy died?" Cleo asked.

"I don't know that we'll ever know for sure, but I talked to Detective Harper again on my lunch break, and we have a theory."

"Oh?" Sam leaned in.

"Cameron apparently had a note in his calendar to call the police first thing Thursday, the day after he was killed. We think he may have believed at first that Bryce killed Darcy, angry about the affair. But something happened on Wednesday, like maybe he noticed a further irregularity in the account, and he got suspicious."

"I could see that," Sam said.

"And then it was just bad luck," I explained. "Cameron

must have run into Harry and, in the course of their conversation, Harry realized that Cameron knew what was going on."

"He was very skilled at reading people," Alice said. "I bet you have to be if you're going to be a successful con man."

"Detective Harper and I have a theory that Harry tried to smooth things over and let on like he didn't know Cameron suspected him. Thanks to the fact that he hung out at the Pit & Pickle all the time, he knew when Cameron would be at the empty fairgrounds Wednesday night. All he had to do was set up his partner to provide an alibi and wait until Eileen left."

Cleo slowly shook her head. "Very sneaky."

"Another clue that I didn't pick up on at the time was when Sam had dropped me off at the front door of the Pit & Pickle and was parking the car," I said. "Harry was waiting for a to-go order and responded when they called out that an order was ready for Jack. He acted like he didn't hear well, and it was loud in there, so I totally ignored it. Later, I realized that if his whole life was running this con in one town and then moving to another town, he probably changed his name every time. Maybe in the last place he ran his scam, he called himself Jack."

"Has Detective Harper learned of other towns where Harry did this?" Cleo asked.

"Not yet, but he's checking," I said. "He has learned, though, that in addition to killing Darcy and Cameron and stealing from the festival, Harry was one of the people responsible for scamming local elderly people with a get-rich-quick deal. And he's caught Harry's accomplice, who was involved in those scams and in making it look like Harry was at the Pit & Pickle when Cameron was killed. It's Harry's cousin, and from the back, he looks exactly like Harry. Add in a recording of Harry talking and it seemed like he was in his car."

Sam pushed up his glasses. "Has he been living with Harry this whole time?"

"No, he was staying at a small cabin outside of town. He and Harry didn't want to be seen together," I said.

"Will the police be able to get the elderly people their money back?" Alice asked.

"Detective Harper's working on it. Some of the money is gone. Harry spent it on living expenses while he was here in Dogwood Springs. But the festival committee had a quick meeting earlier this afternoon and agreed that some of the proceeds from the festival could be used to help make up the difference if we had a good turnout."

Cleo looked from side to side. "You don't need to worry about that. Harry may have done it for all the wrong reasons, but he sure drew a crowd this year. I've never seen so many people at the festival."

"Or so many specialty food trucks," Alice said. "I even saw one selling Minnesota's Pride ice cream in individual serving cartons. You know, the ones with the little flat wooden spoon?"

"Ice cream?" Sam's eyes lit up. "How about we have ice cream and funnel cake for dessert?"

Alice laid a hand over her stomach. "None for me. You all go ahead, and I'll hold the table."

Funnel cake sounded wonderful. Not only had I spent hours smelling its delicious aroma, but I wanted to support Eileen and her family in their time of loss.

Sam and I agreed to split one, and he left the flavor choice up to me. Then he went off to get ice cream for us, and Cleo, Zeke, and I lined up for funnel cake.

"Libby!" Bryce walked up to us. "I'm glad I saw you. I don't know how to thank you for finding the real killer and for believing in me."

"You're welcome, but..." I glanced over at Cleo and pointed a thumb in her direction. "Cleo's the one who believed in you, even when the evidence against you seemed insurmountable, and I was beginning to have my doubts."

"I should have known," he said softly. He gave Cleo a long look, then quickly patted Bella's head and walked away.

Zeke and I exchanged glances but didn't comment.

"I guess I'd better decide what kind of funnel cake I want," I said. Eventually, even though I was tempted by chocolate funnel cake, as well as the option to have a traditional vanilla covered with apple pie filling and caramel sauce, I stuck with the combination that had caught my eye earlier: vanilla funnel cake with strawberry topping and whipped cream.

Cleo and Zeke opted to split a chocolate one, and Zeke had them add caramel sauce and whipped cream.

With the ice cream Sam was getting, we just might hit a new level of all-out decadence.

Soon we were seated back at our picnic table. Sam had beaten us back and had a brown paper bag in front of him.

"They put our ice cream in here to keep it cool." He tapped the bag. "I told them you all were getting funnel cakes, and they'd heard the line was long."

"It wasn't too bad. What flavor of ice cream did you get?" I asked.

"Vanilla for everyone." He pointed at our funnel cakes. "I had a feeling you all would go crazy with the toppings." He pulled out the single-serving ice cream cups and handed one each to me, Zeke, and Cleo.

"Is this Minnesota's Pride?" I asked. The package didn't look like their cartons.

"That's what the sign on the food truck said," Sam picked up his ice cream. "I—"

My breath caught, and I grabbed his arm. "Sam, look at the label."

He studied the carton. "It's an anniversary edition. That's why it looks different."

"Look at the design in the background. Those faint ivy leaves…"

He looked at the carton, then at me, then at the carton again. "They look a lot like that leaf that Ivy Whitfield used to sign the letter she sent to her friend Emily."

"Not a lot like them." I traced the outline of one with my fingers. "Exactly like them."

Cleo let out a squeal. "You mean—"

I nodded. "I mean I think I know what happened to Ivy Whitfield. We knew she married a dairy farmer and helped out on the farm. What if that farm eventually became the dairy that makes Minnesota's Pride ice cream?"

"Oh, my goodness!" Laughter bubbled out of Alice. "You've done it, Libby. You've solved the mystery of what happened to Ivy Whitfield."

"She had such a horrible experience," I said. "Having her father embezzle from the local bank, having her father and stepmother try to marry her off against her will to a rich, older man whose money could have hidden the crime, and then learning that they were willing to pretend she died in a bank robbery in order to save face in the community."

"But she didn't let it ruin her life, did she?" Sam scooped up a big spoonful of ice cream.

"Nope, she didn't." I raised my ice cream cup. "Here's to Ivy, a woman who moved to a new town, built a new life for herself, and may have helped her new husband make their business into such a success that it's Sam's favorite food."

We all laughed.

My heart tingled with excitement. "First thing Monday morning, as soon as Minnesota's Pride opens, I'm going to call them and see if I can talk to one of Ivy's descendants!"

My friends raised their ice cream cups, and we all cheered.

# Chapter Twenty-Three

THE CROWD at the festival was even bigger the next morning. Rodney and I were manning the museum's tent for the day. He was more introverted than Imani or me, but he seemed delighted to talk with visitor after visitor about the displays at our tent.

When he and I were both busy, Bella served as a deputy staff member, greeting visitors and keeping people happy if they had to wait. By eleven, though, even she had gotten tired and was lounging behind the display tables.

And Rodney and I had almost run out of entry forms for our guess-the-antiques contest and the brochures with the form to sign up as annual members of the museum—or lifetime members if someone was feeling especially generous.

Imani was working at her husband's woodworking tent, Alice and a crew of volunteers were staffing the museum, which had its own deluge of tourists who had been to the festival on Friday and decided to stop at the museum before going back to the festival for lunch and an afternoon and evening of shopping and live music. My other board members were either on the festival steering committee, regular volunteers at the festival, or, in the case of one member who said crowds gave him a rash, hiding away at a friend's out-of-town cabin until the festival ended.

In desperation, I called Sam.

He gladly agreed to go by the museum to pick up more brochures and a new stack of entry forms that a volunteer was copying and cutting with our big paper cutter.

At a quarter of twelve, he appeared at the edge of the tent with his arms full. "I had to park in a grassy area past the barns. The stage lot and the main lot are parked under. The guy who directed me said they may have to start turning people away. There's never been such a crowd." He set the boxes of brochures and two plastic grocery bags full of entry forms on a corner of the display table and gave Bella a quick scratch between the ears.

"Sylvia stopped by half an hour ago," I said. "She got about four hours of sleep last night. Apparently, there were numerous crises because of Harry's lack of attention to detail and the fact that lots of volunteers were doing jobs with no training."

"I can only imagine," Sam said.

Rodney stepped closer. "Sylvia's got it under control though. She's even got all the queen contestants and their friends passing out coupons and marketing fliers for the vendors in the less desirable spots. She's bound and determined that every visitor and every vendor here will have the best Dogwood Festival ever."

"Well, we're certainly impressed." A woman who looked to be in her late fifties stepped up to the museum's tent.

She had chin-length dark hair and wore cropped navy pants and a floral sweater. Her face seemed vaguely familiar, but I couldn't place her. I was almost sure I'd never met the man with her, who was nearly bald, short, and round, with a Santa-style white beard and mustache.

"I'm so glad you're enjoying the festival. Would you like to try to guess the antiques?" I gestured to the three items on display.

"Actually, we came to see you," the woman said. "I want you to meet someone." She called to someone at a nearby tent selling silver and turquoise jewelry. They turned and walked toward us.

I gasped. Except for a purple stripe in her hair, the long, feathery earrings, and the fact that she wore ripped jeans and a tie-dyed T-shirt instead of a demure dress, the girl looked exactly like Ivy Whitfield. Same brown hair and dark eyes, same nose, and same chin.

"I'd like you to meet Ariel Olsen, Ivy Whitfield's great-great-great-granddaughter. And I'm one of Ivy's great-granddaughters, Coralee Compton," the woman said.

"When—but how—where—" I sputtered.

"What Libby means is 'Welcome to Dogwood Springs,'" Sam said.

"Yes, of course," I said. "Welcome. I can't tell you how delighted I am to meet you. Are you—I know this may seem crazy—but are you connected in any way to the Minnesota's Pride ice cream company?"

Coralee glanced over at the man who resembled Santa and grinned. "I'm the CEO, and my husband, Albert, here, is the CFO."

Delight zinged through my chest, and I looked at Sam. We'd been right. That drawing on the anniversary ice cream cartons was the same as the drawing Ivy had used to sign her letters to her friend. "How did you find us here at the festival?"

"We stopped by the museum. A woman named Alice told us you'd be here. We did call a few days ago, but she said you didn't know we were coming. Is that right?"

I mentally kicked myself. I should have found that volunteer Andrea and asked her to think hard, to see if there was anything more she hadn't written down. But I'd been so busy with the festival and the murders that I hadn't even thought of it. "I got part of a message, only enough to know that the social media posts had worked, and someone recognized Ivy."

"As soon as she saw that picture on Facebook, Coralee was so excited that we made plans to drive down. The festival threw us for a bit of a loop. We had to stay two towns down the highway because everything was booked, but she was determined to come here and see that painting."

"Did Alice show it to you?" I asked.

"She did indeed." Coralee beamed. "I can't believe it. I got involved in genealogy early this spring, and I'd run into a real roadblock with Great-Grandma Ivy. I couldn't figure out where she'd come from."

"We can tell you the whole story," Sam said. "Or at least what we know of it."

"Libby, I can manage things here." Rodney angled his head toward the line forming behind Coralee and Albert, people who wanted to guess the antiques and see the exhibits from the museum. "You all go have lunch together."

"Thank you, Rodney. I promise I'll fill you in on all the details."

"I'd expect no less," he said.

"Would you mind if Bella came along?" I gestured to her.

She trotted over, eager to be included.

Coralee, Albert, and Ariel quickly agreed, and Bella made three new friends. We headed off to find lunch, with Bella trotting along beside us, tail wagging.

Fifteen minutes later, after Albert insisted on buying our meals, we sat down in a group of picnic tables near the main parking lot, far enough from the stage that we could all converse easily. Bella and Ariel had really taken to each other, and Bella flopped on the grass near her feet.

Sam and I explained about how he'd found the painting in the attic at Ashlington, how my grandmother had bought it at a church bazaar, and how we'd learned that Ivy had been painted out of the portrait. After Sam had the painting restored, we'd gone through early photos from the town school and found Ivy's name. In time, after finding her grave in the local cemetery and reading about how she was supposedly shot by a robber at her father's bank, we'd figured out that the story of her death was all a lie. She'd run away to avoid a marriage her father and stepmother were trying to force her into and ended up on a train to St. Louis. A chance meeting led her to move to a town where she married a man named Thomas.

"Thomas Olsen," Coralee said. "My great-grandfather."

"And he ran a dairy?" Sam asked.

"He did indeed. It was a fairly small business until he married Ivy. In addition to raising four children, she became a driving force behind the dairy's success. She was the person who first encouraged Thomas to start making ice cream, and she came up with the original recipes for the chocolate and vanilla."

"For which I am forever grateful." Sam's voice rang with reverence.

I chuckled. "Sam might be your company's biggest fan. He eats at least a carton a week."

"Usually two," he admitted.

"I knew I liked you," Albert said with a laugh.

I turned to Coralee. "Tell me more about Ivy."

"She was a wonderful woman. She died in 1975 when I was ten, so I remember her well. I even remember her telling me again and again that I could be anything I wanted to be, even the president of Minnesota's Pride. 'The '70s,' Ivy always said, 'were an amazing time for women.'"

As a historian, I could certainly see how a woman born in 1887 would have been amazed at the opportunities women had by the 1970s. In Ivy's lifetime, women had gotten the vote, entered hundreds of fields that had been off-limits when she was a girl, and gone from being virtually excluded from higher education to earning almost half the bachelor's degrees awarded.

"She was right on the cutting edge, advocating for the dairy to start making ice cream," Ariel said. "Back then, of course, we weren't Minnesota's Pride. It was the Olsen Dairy. We didn't become Minnesota's Pride until 1946 when the vanilla ice cream won a blue ribbon at the state fair. But back in the 1920s, ice cream went through a huge boom."

A memory from a college history course bubbled up in my brain. "Because of Prohibition, right?"

"You've got it!" Albert said. "People stopped spending money on alcohol and shifted that money to buying things like ice cream floats at the soda fountain."

"In the 1930s, we started distributing to grocery stores. More people had refrigerators with freezers at home by then," Coralee added. "Thomas was a wonderful dairyman, but Ivy was the marketing brain, the reason Minnesota's Pride is the nationally known brand it is today."

"Which is why you put the ivy leaves on the anniversary cartons," I said.

Coralee and Albert nodded, and I explained how we'd seen them the previous evening and I'd planned to call their office Monday morning.

Sam ran a hand over his mouth. "I can't believe all these months we've been talking about Ivy, researching Ivy, and wondering what became of Ivy after she left Dogwood

Springs, and the whole time we've been eating the ice cream she created."

Ariel nudged Coralee. "Tell them the surprise," she whispered loud enough that we could hear.

Coralee chuckled. "All right, Miss Eager." She looked at Sam and me. "With your approval, we'd like to make a contribution to expand your museum display about Ivy to tell about her life after she left the area. And Minnesota's Pride is going to bring out a new flavor next year. We're calling it Dogwood Springs Delight. We want the two of you to help us figure out what flavor it will be. We'll come up with three test flavors, have them shipped overnight in dry ice to you, and you can choose the one you like best."

Laughter bubbled out of me, and I pressed a hand over my heart. "We'd be thrilled to expand the display." One more way for visitors to the museum to see how fascinating the past was and—if they enjoyed ice cream—how much it affected our lives today. I looked over at Sam. "And I can't imagine anything better than a Dogwood Springs ice cream flavor."

We finished eating, talking a mile a minute about Ivy and ice cream flavors, and I reluctantly headed back to the museum's tent, knowing Rodney needed a chance to have lunch as well.

Coralee, Albert, and Ariel walked back with us, and I

arranged to meet them after lunch the next day, once the festival had ended, to show them the letters the museum had on display from Ivy and a photo I had of the family portrait before it had been restored. I'd drive them by the place where Ivy's home had stood, by the bank her father had owned—now majorly updated—and take them to the cemetery to see her fake grave. With luck, we'd even be able to stop by and meet the descendants of Ivy's best friend, Emily.

"I can't thank you enough." Coralee drew me into a hug. "The work you've done researching Ivy's history means the world to me." She squeezed my arm, then hugged me once more, and Albert and Ariel hugged me as well. They all petted Bella and told her goodbye, then shook hands with Sam and Rodney, who said he was going to take Sam with him while he got his lunch because he couldn't wait to hear the whole story.

After promises to meet at the museum on Sunday, they finally walked away.

Sam gave me a huge kiss of congratulations, but, when crowds thronged the museum tent wanting to know what had happened, eventually went off with Rodney.

And I explained, again and again, to festivalgoers about the famous Clayton Smithton portrait, which we now knew included the woman behind Minnesota's Pride ice cream, on display at the museum. I took in dozens of guesses about the antiques, received five annual membership forms with money collected by credit card, and answered endless questions about the museum.

The last tourist wandered away, and I collapsed into a folding chair.

"Quite the center of attention, aren't you, Libby?"

My heart tightened, and I turned to face my ex-husband, Reggie.

~

"Reggie." I stood. I'd completely forgotten he planned to visit Dogwood Springs this weekend. "You're here for the festival."

I smoothed my hair and looked at the man who had once been my whole world. Of course, that was before he cheated on me, divorced me, and worked things so I lost my job at the prestigious Swarthmore House in Philadelphia.

In a way, Reggie was inadvertently responsible for me moving to Dogwood Springs, back when the director's position here in town was the only museum job I could get.

Although he still had the same pale blond hair and gray eyes and wore a light blue polo shirt that I'd bought for him when we were married, he seemed different. Was it my imagination or did he look older, even a little jowly, and thicker around the middle? Or had he always looked that way and I was now comparing him to Sam?

Reggie leaned in for what had to be the most awkward hug ever.

As soon as was even remotely polite, I stepped back. Maintaining professional ties was one thing. Hugging was another.

Reggie didn't seem to notice my discomfort, but Bella did, and she wriggled between us.

"Oh," I glanced down at her. "This is Bella, my dog."

Reggie stepped back. "You know I'm allergic," he said.

I did, and I could understand why he didn't pet her. I could even understand why he might not talk to her, thinking—correctly—that if he showed her any attention, she'd soon cover his pants with dog hair. But did he have to look at her with such disdain?

I stroked her back, letting her know that I, for one, loved her dearly.

"I stopped by the museum earlier, and a woman named Alice told me how to find you here." Reggie shook his head. "You must be doing a great job. She told me she's president of the museum's board of directors, and she couldn't stop singing your praises."

Delight rippled through my chest. Once again, Alice was a gem.

"I didn't mean to eavesdrop," he said. "But I heard what you were telling people about that Clayton Smithton painting you've got on display and the Minnesota's Pride connection. That's a hugely profitable company. How much are you going to try to get from them?"

I blinked. "We didn't discuss numbers." I'd been so excited to learn what happened to Ivy and meet her descendants that I hadn't even thought about trying to take advantage of their generosity. Count on Reggie, though, to cut right to the cash.

"That Clayton Smithton painting's a loaner, right?" The

sun glinted off Reggie's hair, which I would swear was thinner now than it had been when we were married.

"No, it was given to the museum. How, uh, how are you doing these days?"

"Not as well as you." He shook his head, then pasted on a smile I knew was fake. "I'm happy for you, Libby, but the Swarthmore House has been having financial difficulties. We've had to cut back a lot. Felicity even lost her job."

With difficulty, I refrained from pointing out the irony. Felicity was the woman Reggie had left me for, the woman years younger than me—and nowhere nearly as qualified—who'd ended up with the job that used to be mine.

"She moved out to Phoenix. The two of us are over."

"I'm sorry," I said, not feeling sorry at all. "That has to be hard for you."

"Yeah. I should have known you'd understand. You always did understand me better than anyone." Reggie stepped closer.

I edged back. My ability to understand him ended the day I found out he was cheating on me.

Seeing him again, though, wasn't as bad as I'd feared. I'd dreaded his visit, thinking I'd feel all stressed. Instead, I was riding high on the interest in the museum at the festival and the incredible news about Ivy.

Oh, I had wanted Reggie to see me as successful in my career, but now that it had happened, now that I saw him more clearly, I realized that his opinion didn't matter anymore. In a weird way, I almost felt grateful to him. Back at the Swarthmore, I'd been one of many workers, simply another cog in the machine. Here in Dogwood Springs, I was the director of the local history museum, the person in charge, and a vital member of the community. Here, in this little Missouri town where I hadn't wanted to move, I mattered.

"Reinforcements have arrived!" Rodney exclaimed as he stepped into the tent from the side.

"And I brought you an iced tea." Sam walked up and handed me a cup.

"Hi, guys. This is Reggie, my ex-husband, who works at the Swarthmore, the house museum where I used to work back in Philadelphia." I gestured. "Reggie, this is Rodney, the curator at our local museum."

I gestured to Sam. "And this is Sam Collins, the man I've been seeing. He teaches computer science at the local university, and he created Dinner Zapp."

Sam looked at me and raised an eyebrow. Then he shot a glance at my ex and, as if he'd somehow picked up on the awkwardness of the moment, drew himself up to where he was a good six inches taller than Reggie.

"The students get a kick of out my stories about the little tech firm I ran in California," Sam said. There was something about the way he pronounced the word *little* that made it clear it was anything but.

"Dinner Zapp?" Reggie looked at Sam. "Seeing each other?"

"Yep." Sam slipped an arm around my waist.

I studied the two of them, trying to parse the real feelings from the testosterone. Had all my late-night worries about Sam been foolish? Did he really care for me as much as he seemed? Or was this merely an act, a response to the discomfort he sensed I felt around Reggie?

Sam looked over at Reggie. "By the way, did Libby tell you how she just captured a double murderer?"

Reggie's eyes grew wide, and he snickered. "You're kidding, right?"

"Not kidding at all." Rodney stepped to my side. "She figured out who the killer was and brought him to his knees with her pepper spray."

"Libby?" Reggie's voice squeaked. "Caught a murderer?"

Sam, Rodney, and I all nodded.

"Wow. Well, uh, nice seeing you," Reggie muttered as he backed away. "Seems like you've done all right for yourself since you divorced me."

Since *I* divorced *him*? My eyes almost bugged out. I started to protest but thought better of it.

Because, in the end, it didn't matter. Reggie could tell himself whatever lies he wanted. He was no longer part of my life.

I smiled at Rodney and Sam, and when I looked back, Reggie was gone.

And a new crowd of visitors was swarming the museum's tent.

Sam quickly told me he'd be back at my dinner break, and I turned to face the crowd. A few more hours manning the tent, and then he and I would have time alone, time when I needed to get some straight answers.

## Epilogue

AFTER WE ATE that night in the wine and beer garden, Sam and I got up to give our table to another couple.

"C'mon, Bella." Sam clapped his hand against his thigh.

Bella gave her whole body a good shake, and her ears perked up, ready to explore.

The evening was balmy, and I gazed about, looking at the tents filled with shoppers, the lines at the food trucks, and the lovely setting of dogwood trees.

The three of us walked all around the festival, starting near the stage, where the headliner for the whole weekend, an up-and-coming indie band from Kansas City, was warming up. The mic crackled with feedback, and the lead singer ran through part of a song. Even that tiny sampling sounded fabulous to me. From the size of the crowd spread out in lawn chairs and on blankets, I wasn't the only one looking forward to the evening's entertainment.

We strolled up and down each row of the vendor tents,

food trucks, and exhibits. Even though I'd previously walked past all the vendors, I was amazed at the quality and variety of handcrafted items for sale—from hand-woven blankets to beaded wrap bracelets to decorated, personalized cowboy hats. And although—or perhaps because of the fact that—there were only a few hours left in the festival, shoppers seemed eager to make last-minute purchases. At JoBeth's tent, Bella stopped and looked longingly. I bought another six homemade dog biscuits to dole out over the next few days. Then Sam, Bella, and I continued on. I caught the aroma of fried pickles, then the scent of cotton candy, and finally, the irresistible smell of deep-fried pralines.

Sam and I each had one, but they didn't last long, and after we finished, our hands were covered in chocolate and caramel. I had to go back and grab more napkins for us.

"Do you have time to walk a little farther?" He wiped his hands and tossed his napkin in a nearby trashcan.

I checked my phone. "Fifteen more minutes before I said I'd be back to the museum tent to help Imani."

"Let's head over there." He pointed to a small grove of dogwood trees.

"Sure," I agreed, but my chest tightened. This was the time. If I was going to be truly comfortable in my relationship with Sam, I needed to ask him a question.

I knew I never wanted to go back to Reggie. That chapter of my life was over. With luck, after seeing him today, I could move on with one less trunk of emotional baggage. But some of the wounds from that relationship were still healing. Some of the things Reggie said during our divorce had cut deep into my self-esteem, been internalized, and would take more time to get past. I couldn't take a chance of feeling deceived again. I had to have things out in the open.

A minute later, Sam stopped in the middle of a grove of dogwoods. The trees weren't as tall as the oaks that filled the forests around Dogwood Springs, but they rose to about thirty feet and surrounded us like a cloud. In the golden light of the setting sun, the white blossoms looked almost magical, and the melodies of the indie band mixed with the calls of nearby birds. If I was ever going to have a private moment to talk with Sam at the festival, this was it.

I gazed at him, taking in the strong line of his jaw, his broad shoulders, and the way his black-framed glasses made him look even sexier. His good looks made starting this conversation even more difficult.

But I drew in a deep breath, steeled myself for what I didn't want to hear, and turned to face him. "Are you moving back to California? Or anywhere away from Dogwood Springs?" I spoke quickly, wanting to get this discussion over with. If things were ending between us, I needed to know.

Sam ran a hand through his hair, leaving it rumpled, and his face scrunched up. "Moving?"

"That night we had Mexican takeout at your house. I didn't mean to eavesdrop, but I heard you on the phone. It sounds like you're starting a new company."

His face eased.

Was that good? Or was he relieved to finally tell me?

"Libby." He stepped closer to me. "I'm not going anywhere. I am starting a new little venture, just something to keep my mind occupied when grading gets boring, but it will all be online, and I plan to run it from Ashlington. I wasn't trying to hide anything from you. I was going to tell you once I had my branding options back from the marketing team. I wanted to get your opinion on their ideas."

I covered my mouth with both hands, then let them fall to my sides. "I'm so glad. I—I had a bit of late-night paranoia the other day and was afraid you might be leaving town and ending things with me."

"Never! And *you* had paranoia?" Sam's voice sounded scratchy. "Think how I felt when I walked up and saw you talking to your ex-husband. That's why I wanted to come over here, so I could talk to you alone and make sure I read the situation correctly when I thought you wanted him to leave. Did you?"

"Yes!" I said as my breath rushed out. "I have no interest in ever getting back together with Reggie."

Sam's shoulders eased, and he slid his arms around my waist. "And I have no interest in ever moving away from you." He pulled me closer. "I love you, Libby."

My mouth fell open, and tingles shot down my arms, like bubbles bursting inside my skin. I'd never dreamed our conversation would end like this. "Oh, Sam, I love you too!"

He pulled me closer and traced one finger down my cheek.

My heart rate sped, and a wave of warmth swirled through my chest.

"My beautiful, amazing Libby," Sam whispered.

I raised a shaking hand and threaded my fingers into his hair.

And he leaned down and kissed me.

When at last I stepped back and opened my eyes, the grove of dogwood trees spun around me. My heart felt so full that I thought it might burst. Sam Collins was in love with me. Sam Collins! A man who was so good-looking and so successful that I still couldn't believe he'd ever looked in my direction.

And yet...

He. Had.

The pain of my past was slowly fading. Bit by bit, I was moving on. I felt stronger, proud of my professional accomplishments, and proud that this time I'd picked a man who was not a liar, not a sneak, not a cheater. Though I'd never expected it when I moved here, I'd found a rewarding career, dear friends, and a wonderful man, all in the little town of Dogwood Springs.

Bella nuzzled my leg, reminding me that I'd also found the sweetest, most loving, most intelligent dog around. I bent down, scratched between her ears, and told her that I loved her too.

"One thing does disappoint me, though," Sam said.

A niggle of worry slithered back in and pricked at my heart. I stood up. "What?"

"I really liked working with you to learn what happened to Ivy. I'm going to miss our historical sleuthing."

My worry dissolved into a chuckle. "That won't be a problem."

"You think we'll have more historical mysteries to solve?"

"I can almost guarantee it. That's the beauty of history. There's always more to uncover."

"You'll let me help?" Sam asked.

"I wouldn't have it any other way."

He grinned, and I pulled him back down for another kiss.

Another historical mystery was waiting for us, right around the corner. I could just feel it.

With luck, we could solve it, like we solved the mystery of what happened to Ivy Whitfield.

And if, by chance, another murder took place in Dogwood Springs, I knew my friends and I—and Bella— would do our best to solve it as well.

My future in Dogwood Springs beckoned, and I couldn't wait to see how my relationship with Sam might develop and discover what adventures lay ahead.

**Thank you for reading this book!**

**Are you ready to return to Dogwood Springs for another cozy mystery?** Join Libby, Bella, and their friends in the next book in the series where Sam and Libby begin investigating another historical mystery and the team is drawn into another murder!

## Amid a century of styles, a historic fashion show turns fatal.

Libby Ballard couldn't be more pleased. What could be more charming than hosting a historic fashion show as a special event for the museum she runs in the small town of Dogwood Springs, Missouri? But when tragedy strikes and a spiteful local figure is found dead backstage, the curtain rises on a mystery of murderous proportions.

When the police spotlight a suspect who Libby knows is innocent, she realizes she must step in to catch the true culprit and protect the reputation of her beloved museum, already strained by connection to previous murders. With strong determination, a keen eye for detail, and her trusty golden retriever, Bella, by her side, she embarks on a journey through a labyrinth of lies and long-held grudges.

But the suspects are many, the truth is elusive, and the specter of danger lurks in every shadow. Can Libby outwit the killer before another victim falls?

If you like a cozy mystery with a pet who will win your heart, friends who feel like family, and a hint of romance, you'll love *Hemlines, Handbags & Havoc.*

**Don't miss your free reader bonuses!** Join Sally's cozy mystery newsletter to:

- download the free five-chapter prequel to the Dogwood Springs series, BED & BREAKFAST & BURGLARY
- read exclusive bonus content for every book, such as a scene in Bella's point of view
- learn about new releases, and more!

Visit Sally's website at www.sallybayless.com/free-mystery/ to join.

**See all the books in the Dogwood Springs Cozy Mystery Series** at www.sallybayless.com.

# Acknowledgments

This book was so much fun to write! I had a blast thinking about the food, music, and crafts that would surround Libby, Bella, and their friends as they investigated a murder at the Dogwood Festival. A big thanks to my dear friend, Martha Burton Long, who helped me research local festivals so I could make this book more real.

Once I had the basic story down, I sent it to my beta reading team—Betsy Anderson, Debbie Edwards, Barbara Hackel, Janice Huwe, Martha Burton Long, and Kim Lyons. They asked so many great questions and really helped refine the story. Thank you, beta readers. You play such a vital role!

A big shout out to my fellow author Cathryn Brown, my writing accountability partner who is always there to help when I run into trouble with a plot or other issues. I'm so glad you're in my writing world!

I also want to give a big thank you to Donna Lynn Rogers of DLR Cover Design. After I saw the gorgeous cover you created based on my synopsis, I was even more inspired to write this book. That cover just makes me happy whenever I look at it!

I am also so grateful to my family, like my son, Michael,

who helps me with tech issues. While this book was in production, I shifted from a PC to a Mac system, and you made the transition much easier. My daughter, Laurel, is always so encouraging and offers great insight whenever I need to bounce ideas off someone. And, as with each of my books, my husband Dave was my first reader, the one who cheered me on when things were going well, and the one who cheered me up when I faced difficulties. Thank you, thank you, wonderful, supportive family!

Finally, I want to thank each and every person who reads my books. I am delighted that you choose to spend time with me in the little town of Dogwood Springs. And to those readers who I get to know better through my news-letter and social media, the ones who reach out, interact, help me name characters, and laugh with me, I say a special thank you. You brighten my days!

If, in spite of help from editors, beta readers, and my advance reader team, errors slipped by, please know that any mistakes are mine alone.

## About the Author

After many years away, Sally Bayless lives in her hometown in the Missouri Ozarks. She's married and has two grown children. When not working on her next book, she enjoys reading, BBC mysteries, word puzzles, swimming, and shopping for cute shoes.